SHILLING & FLORIN

BOOK FOUR:
THE CASE OF SILVER & SOVEREIGN

KATE HALEY

ISBN: 978-1-991364-08-1 (paperback)
978-1-991364-07-4 (kindle)
978-1-991364-19-7 (hardcover)

Cover design by Kate Haley

*Thank you to the fans keeping
Shilling & Florin alive*

CONTENTS

Visit **www.katehaleyauthor.com** for deals and current news from the author.

1

The shot rang through the air, clean and crisp. There was fog settling around the hills, and wisps of cloud clung to the greenery in the distance. A colossus of a man with dark hair lowered his rifle. His companion sniffed.

"Good shot," he complimented the other man.

"Hgh," the shooter grunted, still staring into the distance. He set the rifle on his shoulder and began to walk away. "Don' bother me with petty li'l details now. Just get it done."

"Aye," the other man agreed, tagging nervously behind, like he wasn't sure if he should be following or leaving.

"Aye indeed," the shooter warned. "I'm payin' ya to teach that boy a lesson. Make sure it's one he ain't ever gonna forget."

The other man stopped, nodding, and swallowed nervously. That was a dismissal, for sure. But part of his brain, the part that knew that if he was wrong the shooter could gun him down out here without anyone ever finding him again, hesitated. The man with the rifle paused to glance over his shoulder. He looked back with eyes that were not the eyes of a patient man. More the dark and bloodshot eyes of a demon.

The sun was out but the air had a chill. If Amy had been in charge of her own recovery, she would have been out experiencing the day and trying to get her strength back, but the doctor overseeing her recuperation was a friend of her father's and everything had to be taken slowly and gently so that she didn't break. Being a lady was awful. She wasn't even allowed to spit in anyone's face for treating her like a doll.

Things had been tense and painful, and she wasn't even sure the worst of it was her physical recovery. She had wished she could think of something other than Charlie, and the anger that plagued her when she saw him now. The anguish. Her birth father, Argent, had written to her of the incident. Of course it had been in the newspapers. Of course he had read them. He was deeply concerned about her and Amy had been forced to send a hurried reply that he not come and visit yet. She just needed a bit of time but hoped she would see him again soon. God, she had no idea if she'd managed to be polite about it, but she had tried.

That had led to her having to admit to her to other father, Henry, that she had inadvertently found her birth father and then not told him. He was taking it in stride, but it was so hard to tell with him sometimes. Henry was so proper. So reserved. He had been through so much recently… sometimes it felt like he was coping by cutting himself off from emotion.

All of that had snowballed into a lingering guilt that she carried too for her mother's letter. The secret letter she had found in her bag on the way home from France that she hadn't told anyone about. The letter that had left her weeping like a child and still brought a pained lump to her throat. The only thing in her life that she'd ever had signed 'mum'. The letter that told her she could always rely on Charlie. It made her want to try cathartic violence.

She couldn't even distract herself with the publication of her book. Her very own Dawson & Kropp had hit the shelves, safely under the penname Florence Pound… which felt a little bit easy to decipher, but should suffice. As long as no one ever looked too closely. The whole point of the pen name was to hide her identity, even from her loved ones — especially from her loved ones! — whom she did not want to know that she had written a Dawson & Kropp book. So that was just another thing she had to hide now, on top of everything else. The only person who knew about it was Charlie… which brought her back to square one and the cathartic violence.

At least today came with distractions. Good company and entertainment — and no one was trying to keep her in bed anymore. Those days, thank goodness, were behind them. Today she was taking tea in the parlour with Laura and Jane, who were planning for their wedding and pretending to seek input.

"We don't want a big wedding," Laura was saying graciously. "Just a small, intimate gathering."

"Of over a hundred people..." Jane muttered.

"A hundred?!" Amy blurted.

"That's small!" Laura insisted. "I've told you, darling, if you want smaller, you have to say. I'm happy to compromise, but you have to ask. You can't just be sarcastic."

Jane rolled her eyes, but her discreet smile suggested she was needling her fiancée for fun.

"Besides," Laura huffed, "nearly half of that is my family. There's a lot of them. They're crazy. I've got five sisters in my bridal party alone..."

"But I imagine you're trying to keep them as far from the planning as possible...?" Amy replied, remembering Laura's sisters with some apprehension.

"It's one of the reasons we've come to you," Jane agreed. "Actually, Amy... we were wondering..."

"What's this 'we' business?" Laura demanded.

"*We*," Jane leant on the word. "*We* were wondering, but also specifically I was wondering, if... if you would be interested in being my maid of honour...?" Jane trailed off nervously, casting repeated glances at Amy's impassive expression before turning her eyes to her fidgeting fingers.

Amy reached out with a smile and placed her hand over Jane's.

"Jane, I would be delighted," she replied.

Jane grinned back, a proper beaming smile of gratitude. Laura was giving them a smug side-eye, as though she'd verbally anticipated this result.

"And you can bring Shilling as your date," she proposed.

Amy's mood instantly fell, and she was too weak to hide it in her face. Laura was too busy with her cheeky insinuations to notice, but Jane caught it instantly.

"What's wrong?" she asked.

Once attention had been drawn, Laura caught on quickly, snapping her attention back.

"Oh no," she lamented. "You don't have to bring him! You don't have to bring anybody! The wedding can be a date-free zone for you! That would be totally fine!"

"What did he do this time?" Jane sighed. She traced a finger up the vase of the large centrepiece bouquet on the table. "I thought you said these were from him?"

"They are," Amy sighed. "He dropped them off this morning."

"And said something stupid?" Laura commiserated, her eyes huge with sympathy. "Is it just a boy thing? Everyone knows boys say stupid things all the time. It might not be as bad as you think."

"He didn't say anything stupid," Amy sighed. "He barely talks to me at all. He comes by every two days like clockwork, with fresh flowers, and refuses to meet my eye or come anywhere near me."

"Oh my Mary Magdalene!" Laura exclaimed. "Is he trying to court you? Officially?!"

"No," Amy glowered. "He's trying to avoid me, but I think guilt is getting in the way. So he comes by to bring flowers, but he won't even come close enough to entertain the idea of a private conversation. He just hangs about in the doorway. Sometimes he hands the flowers to Digby at the front door and leaves without saying hello."

"What does your father make of it?" Jane asked. "I can't imagine he'd be well pleased with a man messing you about."

"Oh, Daddy heartily approves and thinks Charlie's being a gentleman," Amy huffed. "I want to hit them both with a skillet."

"I'll get you one!" Laura offered, starting to stand.

Jane reached out instantly, catching her and gently guiding her back into her seat.

"I know this might be an unhelpful question," Jane began, "given that you said he won't engage in a private conversation with you, but do you know why he's behaving this way?"

"Because he's an idiot," Amy blushed, turning her face away and trying not to think of any of the other obvious reasons.

"I only ask because we talked a lot in our studies about the importance of healing the mind as well as the body," Jane recalled. "You were seriously wounded and you're healing admirably, but, not that it's my business, I would also diagnose that you were using belittlement and dismissal as healing tactics to try and condense your trauma to a manageable size. I can only imagine what it was like for Shilling to have to live through that as well. Possibly, he has his own issues to work through and is attempting to be caring and respectful the only way he knows how?"

Amy pressed her lips together. It was so hard to argue with Jane. Amy had considered her own reasoning logical, but Jane had the benefit of perspective as well. Of course what she said was true, but she didn't know everything. Amy could still feel the terror that had gripped her when she'd seen Kopeck pull a gun on Charlie. She could still feel the pain of the bullet, the weight of Charlie's body against hers when they had fallen, when he had carried her from the burning church. She could still see the file with the headless body beneath the statue of Justice. She could still taste Charlie on her lips in the hospital room.

"Or is there more than that…?" Jane asked softly, like she was reading her thoughts.

Amy's eyes shot up, glancing at her sharply.

"Ooo!" Laura caught on. "There is something we don't know!"

Amy pouted as she looked away again. Of course they'd caught her. Inevitable. She shook a stray curl back from her eyes and stared out the window. If she didn't say something, they'd start hounding her.

"I kissed him," she muttered at the glass.

"I beg your pardon?" Jane raised an eyebrow.

"I kissed him!" Amy hissed louder. "At the hospital. When I was doped up after surgery. I kissed him and he ran away."

Jane and Laura shared a long look.

"I know," Amy sighed. "But I wasn't myself and he hasn't let me explain. Besides, I think he's trying to distance himself from me in a gross act of misplaced chivalry."

Jane and Laura shared another long look. It was infuriating.

"What… exactly… was the part of that where you

weren't acting as yourself?" Laura asked.

Jane snorted. Amy glared at them. Jane reached out and took her hand.

"Amy, darling," Jane smiled at her. "We know you like him, but, well… he's a bit odd. If his feelings aren't reciprocal, if he's trying to be kind while letting you down gently…"

"Oh, that is not what's happening," Laura countered. "It's Charles Shilling. What are the odds he's ever been kissed by a lady other than Amy? He probably is trying to court you and has no idea how."

"He's not trying to court me!" Amy huffed. "He's trying to abandon me because he's worried I'll get hurt again. Jane's right. He…" she trailed off and thought for a moment, trying not to be irritated at him long enough to empathise with what she knew he'd been through. "Jane's right," she repeated softly. "Charlie… I can't imagine what it was like for him. Everything that happened… it must have been awful. I think if our positions were reversed… how I would feel if I'd watched him take a bullet for me and then had to save his life… and…" she left the sentence hanging. It was no one else's business what else he might have done, and what that said about the state of his mental wellbeing. "I'd probably do anything I could to try and keep him out of danger, but I wouldn't push him away!"

"That's because he is the danger," Laura pointed out. "You've been in nothing but trouble since you started getting tangled with him, but he's probably been safer than usual with someone else watching his back."

"As your friends," Jane began, "could we politely request that you become infatuated with someone a little more reasonable?"

"No," Amy replied.

Laura laughed and hugged her from the side, leaning into her shoulder and embracing her around the neck. She kissed Amy's cheek.

"I love you so much and that is a perfectly valid response," she declared.

Jane rolled her eyes at them, but she'd done her best and there were some people you just couldn't help. Laura was still snuggled comfortably into Amy, holding her supportively.

"Well, if this really is the man for you, let us help you," Laura suggested. "I'm very good at bullying men into doing what I want."

"I don't want to bully him," Amy chuckled at her teasing. "I just… I just want to talk to him. Hopefully I'll get the chance to speak with him tonight. We're actually going to the circus — the Great Livre has an act in it now."

"Oooo!" Laura squealed excitedly. "Circus?!"

"There's one up in Hyde Park," Amy chuckled. "Daddy got tickets and invited Charlie."

"I'm surprised he said yes," Jane commented. "If Shilling really is trying to avoid you, it seems strange that he wouldn't make excuses to decline."

Amy couldn't keep the grim tinge from her smile. "Charlie's doing almost anything Daddy asks at the moment. Partly because Daddy isn't asking too much of him. They're both walking on eggshells around each other."

"Why?" Jane asked suspiciously.

"Can't imagine," Amy lied.

"Aside from them both trying to deal with what happened to you?" Jane raised.

"Well, there is that," Amy agreed, glad that there was a very public obvious answer and trying not to think about the many private and unresolved issues that were piling up.

"About this circus...?" Laura pressed.

Amy laughed. "I'm sure Daddy can organise more tickets. Shall I ask?"

"Please," Laura grinned. "I'm really quite keen on the idea of a show this evening. I've been wanting to see Livre for months! Also, then we will be right there with you to help—"

"You mean stick our noses in," Jane chuckled.

"Well, we can get a first-hand experience of Mister Shilling's strange behaviour and see for ourselves," Laura replied. "Then we can aid your relationship troubles more effectively." She said it with such a conspiratorial tone Amy couldn't help but laugh.

"I love that you're supporting me, but please don't get involved," she begged.

"We promise nothing," Laura grinned.

Amy shook her head helplessly with a small laugh. Jane, for all her sense and reason, was wearing a grin all too similar to Laura's, and there was probably no help for any of them. Certainly not if Amy wasn't going to heed her own wisdom, as she still fully intended to add them to her party for the evening. She just had to hope that the circus was enough of a spectacle to overshadow her own drama.

2

The room above the back of the bakery was warm. Cosy, but bordering on stifling. The shutters were open and sunlight bathed the desk Michael sat at as he perused the infinite flow of information that he collected in letters and notes. Charlie was lying upside down across his bed in the corner of the room. He had his shoes up against the wall and his head hanging off the side. He was making pitiful sounds of boredom that Michael was obviously trying to ignore, much to his annoyance.

"You're a man, not a dog, Sleuth," Michael sighed. "Please stop whining for someone to play with you."

"I'm not whining," Charlie whined.

Michael rolled his eyes. "How'd you get that new bruise?"

"Which one?" Charlie replied.

Michael shook his head ruefully. The look he shot Charlie was cynical but amused. Charlie touched his forehead where he realised an obvious dark blue mark was visible now that his hair was falling back from his face.

"I got this from Jasper's latest trap," he admitted grudgingly.

"I thought you said Jasper wasn't bothering you anymore?" Mike looked at him sharply.

"He wasn't," Charlie sighed. "But alas my beautiful reprieve is over. He's back to his old habits. It was rather abrupt too, which was why I didn't see it coming. I honestly don't know if I'm ever going to understand that one. The mystery of Jasper, in this instance, might be beyond me."

"No mystery is beyond you, Sleuth," Mike reminded. "What changed?"

"Florin…" Charlie muttered.

Now he had Michael's attention. Those sharp, cool eyes watched him through slits of consideration.

"I thought Jasper knew about you and Florin," he commented.

"What?" Charlie wriggled on the bed to get a better look at Michael.

"What do you mean 'what'?" Mike retorted.

"What did you mean?!" Charlie demanded.

"I mean Jasper has eyes and ears and he lives in your house, therefore he must have known for quite some time that you fancy the good doctor," Michael elaborated. "You haven't been subtle about it, Sleuth."

"Amy and I aren't really talking anymore," Charlie muttered, fidgeting with his ring and looking away. "So it's not like you make it sound, Skipp."

"Did Jasper drop something on your head when you told him that?" Mike asked.

Charlie raised a curious eyebrow. He'd always known Michael was smart, it was most of what had drawn them together as friends, but that was impressive discernment. Michael, however, was looking decidedly unimpressed.

"Jasper's more practical than I give him credit for," Michael commented, carefully moving sheets of paper around and scanning them quickly. "And it looks like he and I finally agree on something… even if it's just your atrocious behaviour towards Florin."

"I'm trying to protect her!" Charlie exploded, rolling himself upright on the bed and running his fingers through his messy hair. "She got shot because of me, Skipp. She could have died!"

"And you're really delusional enough to think avoiding her is going to improve anything?" Michael drawled sarcastically, cocking an eyebrow at him.

"She had a normal life before I started messing everything up," Charlie muttered.

Michael leant back in his chair and stopped playing with his notes. He linked his fingers across his stomach and pursed his lips thoughtfully.

"I think it was you who told me once, Sleuth, that normality is an illusion," Mike commented. "She had what she perceived as a normal life until Pound Junior went berserk and started cutting up ladies. Even if it was possible for her to get that sense of normality back, and let's be fair, you don't go back after something like that, would she even want to? Shouldn't it be her choice?"

"I hear you, Skipp," Charlie nodded understandingly. "But I don't trust her to make the right one. The wisest course of action for her now is to settle quietly into medicine and claim her life back. Besides, it's better for Pound's case against Tanner if Amy and I have a professional relationship at best. Libel is always a battle of lies and I'd rather not feed that hawker's papers."

"And have you told her any of that?" Mike asked.

"No…" Charlie muttered, casting his eyes down and fidgeting with his ring again. "No… well… well, it's not that simple…" Charlie could hear Michael rolling his eyes.

"Have you at least spoken to her about the kiss at the hospital?" Michael asked.

Charlie flushed with shame and Michael groaned exasperatedly at him.

"Look, it's easier if I just cut ties, and it's better in the long run," Charlie huffed. "She's mad enough with me as it is, and if Pound stopped bloody guilting me into visiting, this could all blow over. As it is, he seems determined I shouldn't just walk away, which doesn't make any sense! It's the sensible thing to do, and I thought he'd be rather pleased that I wasn't around endangering his daughter, but every time I see him he gives me this look… and I don't know what it means but I've never felt so guilty in my life as when he looks at me now… and every time Amy looks at me it's like she wants to hit me with a skillet. I know she does. I can just tell. There's a skillet-whacking look in her eye."

"You're an idiot," Michael told him bluntly.

"You're not the first person to say that," Charlie sighed, keeling over again. "What's wrong with me, Skipp? I'm either a genius or an idiot. How come there's no middle ground?"

"Because it's about balance, Sleuth," Mike smiled. "You're so brilliant with some things that you have to be a complete imbecile with others to even the scales."

Charlie poked his tongue out at his friend. Michael just grinned like he got enough of that kind of behaviour from his siblings. A small bang came from the landing outside his room, as though someone was knocking about on the stairs outside. Mike startled at the sound, but tried to cover it. Charlie lay with his cheek pressed against the blankets and watched Mike curiously. Skipp kept his eyes on the door a moment, almost hopeful. Then he got back to work with his notes, avoiding Charlie's eye. Charlie got up from the bed slowly, shuffling around until he was sitting on the edge. He set his feet on the floor silently, watching Michael the whole time. Mike didn't look up.

"How long's he been gone?" Charlie asked carefully.

"Just a week," Michael replied with forced nonchalance. There was an underlying tension in his voice that told Charlie it had been a very long week. "He said he had business to sort out of town, so…" The illusion of apathy was shattered by a slight crack in his voice and Mike quickly cleared his throat to cover it. He swallowed uncomfortably and scanned his eyes over more scraps of paper, rearranging them meticulously.

"You know where he is?" Charlie asked.

Michael shook his head. "He took a train north, but I don't know how far." There was a hint of guilt on his tongue, like he was concerned he might be lying. Charlie sighed to himself. It was Mike. He would be trying to be obtuse about the situation, but even if he didn't have all the facts, he wouldn't be able to help having suspicions. "I have to respect his privacy, Sleuth," Michael sighed. "I can't spy on him. He didn't want to tell me where he was going and… and, look, you'd tell me if there was anything I needed to be worried about?"

Charlie pursed his lips in thought. He also didn't know with absolute certainty where Julian had gone. He just had a really, really strong suspicion and could deduce with relative certainty where he was, based on everything he knew about Julian and his situation. Worst case scenario, he could certainly follow after him and find him.

"If I knew anything I thought you needed to know that you didn't…" Charlie began hesitantly.

"I'm not asking you to tell me, Sleuth," Michael sighed. "I know there's things he hasn't told me, and he'll tell me when he's ready. I don't want you to do a Charlie to us. Not unless you absolutely have to."

Charlie nodded. He was pretty sure Mike knew most of the things about Julian that he knew already, even if he was trying to pretend he didn't. After all, half of Charlie's general knowledge came from the titbits Mike picked up from the streets.

"I just…" Michael grimaced. "I just worry about him. I know he didn't want to go, and… it's Julian. He's nearly as good at getting into trouble as you are." Mike gave his paperwork a wry smile and tried to hide the glance he shot at the noise coming and going beyond his door. "Every time I hear someone on the stairs, I think it's him, which I s'pose only serves to prove I'm mad about him."

"Skipp..." Charlie muttered sympathetically. He tossed his hair from his eyes, gazing at his friend empathetically.

The door burst open. Both of them startled as a sleek figure in black appeared in the doorway, leaning in conspiratorially with a mischievous smirk on his face. He leant on the doorhandle and eyeballed them both with a twinkle in his eye.

"Bollocks," he chuckled, "I was really hoping to catch you doing something you shouldn't."

"Julian!" Michael was on his feet and around the desk in seconds.

Julian kicked the door shut behind him as he collided with Michael. The two of them kissed like they hadn't seen each other for years. Their hands were everywhere, in each other's hair and clothes. There were strange but familiar sounds being made that Charlie distinctly recognised.

"I guess that's my cue to—" he stood, eyeing the door behind Julian and trying to calculate how to get through it without disrupting them.

As he edged around them carefully, trying to get to the door, Julian's hand lashed out and caught him by the front of the shirt. Charlie startled. He did not think this was something he was supposed to be included in. Luckily, Julian and Mike untangled from each other just as abruptly as they had collided. Michael looked rather flustered and abashed at his lack of self-control. Julian was still trying to hold onto him with one hand, even as his other slowly released Charlie.

"Where you running, Sleuth?" he grinned. "Can't spare a second for your friend?"

"You didn't look like you had a spare second, Swift," Charlie smiled at him.

"I have an entire spare minute," Julian bragged with a smirk. "Read your girlfriend's new book. It's excellent, by the way. I love her depiction of you."

Charlie cocked his head to the side and stared. He didn't know how to start unpacking everything that was wrong with that statement.

"What's this?" Mike asked.

"Florin's published a Dawson & Kropp under a pen name," Julian smirked. "It's… delightful."

Michael did not manage to stifle his laughter, but he tried. Charlie watched them begrudgingly.

"Florin is not my girlfriend and the book has no references to me whatsoever," he paused a moment and then added with a shrug, "it is good, though."

His friends chose that moment to laugh at him, and he decided that they were monsters who did not need his time or attention. He huffed at them and turned to leave.

"Oh, Sleuth!" Julian called after him gently, a note of apology in his voice.

"It's good to see you safely back, Swift," Charlie conceded. "Skipp was going mad without you. I assume you got your affairs in order?"

"Affairs?!" Julian exclaimed with mock horror, clapping his hands over Mike's ears. "Not in front of —" he stopped with a choked laugh as Michael elbowed him in the stomach and broke free. Julian was still laughing as he tangled Mike in his arms again, refusing to let him get away completely. Michael wasn't really trying. As much as he pretended to resist, he let Julian hold him. Julian rested his grin against Mike's cheek, brushing his lips against the side of his lover's face. "I wouldn't really," he murmured.

"I'm not actually worried," Michael smiled. "Charlie would have warned me."

"After I got done hitting you with a shovel, Swift," Charlie warned. "Not that I'm concerned, being as you're not the type, but if I ever did catch you running around on Skipp, I would smack you upside the head with a blunt instrument."

"Then you're going to love this next bit..." Julian teased, his hands carefully trying to untuck Michael's shirt and find their way underneath.

"I think that's my cue to leave," Charlie replied, turning to the door again.

"You can stay for this part," Julian offered.

Charlie and Michael both made dubious sounds of protest. Julian laughed at them. He let go of Michael. A fleeting, nearly invisible, second of shyness crossed his face as he pushed his long black curls from his eyes. Then he got on one knee.

Charlie gave an involuntary squeal of delight and made himself comfortable where he stood. Michael didn't react at all. The look on his face suggested he knew what was happening, but he had completely frozen up. He wasn't even blinking.

"Mike," Julian began with an uncharacteristic touch of nervousness, "I know I'm a mess, but I gotta do this before you realise you can do better."

Charlie laughed. Michael didn't. Julian rummaged in his pocket.

"I've had my share of troubles," Julian continued, "as you well know, with money and work and bad crowds and the like… but you never gave up on me, Skipp. Not ever. Even when we both know you shoulda. I've never known anyone like you. You helped me get my life on track. You gave me chances I didn't deserve, and now, well… I guess I'm asking for another one…" Julian pulled a Luckenbooth brooch from his pocket.

Charlie could barely contain himself. He wanted to squeal again and squeeze them both, but he knew better than to involve himself in what was very clearly their moment.

"I fixed it, Mikey," Julian told him. "I fixed me, fixed the business, fixed the money… I'm the best I've ever been and it's only because of you. I could only do it because of you and I don't want to do any of it without you ever again…" Julian trailed off. The nerves were really starting to show and Michael still hadn't moved. He was standing like a statue.

Charlie began to feel his stomach sinking. Mike cracked, just the slightest shift in posture, as though he'd started breathing again. He blinked but his eyes were downcast. He motioned numbly at Julian, bidding him stand.

"Get off the floor, Swift," he muttered.

Now it was Charlie's turn to freeze. He wanted to dive in to fix it, but he didn't know what had gone wrong. He looked between them in a panic as Julian got slowly to his feet.

Michael slid his hands around Julian's face, cupping his cheeks, slipping his fingers into Julian's hair and resting his forehead against Julian's. Julian leant into every motion, sneaking his arms around Mike and pulling him close.

"You're such a twat," Mike chuckled.

"If I'm going too fast, Skipp—" Julian whispered.

"You're not going anywhere, Swift," Michael replied, smiling softly. "I can't do better than you, you git."

Julian kissed him, pulling him in tighter still. Michael kissed him back. Charlie watched curiously as the two of them seemed to pick up where they had left off seconds before. He cocked his head to the side and regarded them analytically, trying to deduce whether or not he needed to step in. The two of them staggered across the room together, tangled in each other and leaving a trail of garments in their wake. At the point that trousers were being lost and they were nearing Mike's bed, Charlie decided they had the situation well in hand and fled.

When he was halfway down the stairs he stopped and wondered if he had perhaps bolted too hastily in a panic. He tipped his head to the side again and listened. He decided that he had fled at exactly the appropriate pace, if not a little late.

At the bottom of the stairs, he encountered Terry carrying a tray of freshly baked butter knots. Michael's oldest brother cast an imposing figure in the narrow hallway but Charlie barely noticed. All memories of the morning and past troubles were forgotten as he stared, transfixed, at the passing tray. Terry raised an eyebrow at the noises coming down the staircase.

"Julian's back?" he checked.

Charlie stared. Terry sighed.

"Help yourself, Shilling," he offered ruefully.

Charlie raised a tentative hand and plucked a hot fresh knot from the tray. It was nearly scalding on his fingers, but that wasn't going to stop him as he ripped it open and released a cloud of buttery steam. He breathed deep. Then he shoved a morsel of fluffy, crusty bread in his mouth with a sound that was, if he was being honest, a little too like the sounds from upstairs.

"I love you," he muttered around the bread.

"Don't get any ideas," Terry warned.

"I was talking to the bread," Charlie told him. "Bread is my only real love."

Terry gave him a hopeless grin. "And how's your doctor lady?" he asked.

"She's not bread," Charlie replied, shoving more bread in his mouth.

Terry laughed at him. "Don't let Mike hear you talking like that. I understand he has thoughts on the matter— God almighty!" Terry looked to the ceiling. "Do they have to be so loud?! Thank Christ his bedroom's over the kitchen and not the shop. They'd drive away customers with that racket. They're driving me away and I bloody live here!"

"I'd settle in for the long haul, Terry," Charlie warned, shoving the last of the knot in his mouth. "I think they just got engaged."

Terry raised an eyebrow at him. Charlie did his best earnest look, but was aware that his cheeks were bulging.

"Did they now?" Terry mused. "Well, congratulations to us all. What do you think the odds are they'll get a place of their own?"

"Not high," Charlie replied around his mouthful of bread.

Terry gave him a look of tempered amusement. Charlie wasn't sure if that was because he shouldn't have been talking with his mouth full, or if this had been one of those instances where he was supposed to have made up a lie for the sake of conversation. He wasn't always good at reading those situations. Finally, Terry made a sound halfway between a sigh and a chuckle. He plucked another knot off the tray and held it out.

"Here you go, Shilling."

"'fank you," Charlie replied, taking the bread gratefully and accepting that sticking around for anything else was pushing his luck. The six Pence siblings liked Charlie, and he liked them, but Michael was the only one he was actually friends with, and Michael was presently very occupied. He left out the side door to avoid the shop and sauntered from the alleyway, across the street, and into his house.

The opening of the front door was tentative, to say the least, but there were no notable traps from Jasper waiting for him. He moved as silently and carefully as he could into the house and up the first flight of stairs to his room. Before he touched the doorhandle, he knew something was wrong. The way the door was sitting wasn't right. The crack beneath it dimmed. There was something heavy on the other side waiting to collide with him, or fall on him, or get destroyed by him opening the door. He considered it for a second, and then turned and continued up the stairs, still eating his second knot. He did not have the energy to deal with whatever was waiting to ambush him.

Instead, he continued on to Rebecca's living room. The door there stood wide open and his sister was inside. She sat at her sewing station, embroidering a dress and humming to herself. Her face lit up when he appeared in the doorway.

"Good morning, Charlie," she smiled. "I thought you were out."

"I was," Charlie replied, shoving the last of the second knot in his mouth.

Rebecca gave him a reproving look and he knew that one was for talking with his mouth full. He had been on the receiving end of that look many times before. It wasn't one he heeded. He outstared her, chewing slowly and brushing the last dusty crumbs of flour from his fingers.

"And how are the Pence children?" she relented, turning back to her sewing and ignoring his behaviour.

"Good," Charlie answered, strolling by various armchairs and eyeing them for optimum available comfort. "Michael and Julian just got engaged, I think."

"Really?" Rebecca exclaimed. "That's wonderful. Pass on my congratulations when next you see them."

Charlie gave a grunt of agreement and flopped into

an armchair, settling comfortably.

"And how's Florin?" Becky coaxed.

Charlie glowered. He knew she'd waited until he was settled and wasn't just going to turn around and walk out to avoid the question.

"How's Florin, Charlie?" Becky pressed.

"She's recovering well…" he muttered reluctantly.

"I heard you're going to the circus with her and Henry tonight," Becky continued to lead the conversation.

Charlie regretted sitting down. He should have just walked into Jasper's trap instead. A bucket of mop water on the head might not be so bad about now.

"Pound insisted," he admitted. "I… I'm not sure it's a good idea… but he… he insisted."

"You'll have a good time, Charlie," Rebecca encouraged. "It will be good for you to get out with friends and do something that isn't work." She eyed him, taking in his posture and expression with a sigh. "Would it really be so terrible to spend an evening with them?"

"No… no, of course not," Charlie muttered, curling into himself. "No. No, there's… there's just the libel case to consider…"

"A lawsuit I'm sure Lord Pound has well in hand," Becky reminded. "It might even help the case to have the two of you seemingly interact as normal, rather than behaving like you have something to hide."

Charlie nodded. It was not a nod of agreement and it very much lacked enthusiasm.

"Charlie," Rebecca sighed sympathetically. "You're

being an idiot."

"Why do people keep saying that?" he pondered.

"The woman took a bullet for you and you won't even talk to her," Becky rebuked. "Women who take bullets for you, Charlie, are not doing it so that you will start avoiding them thereafter with oceans of misplaced guilt."

"I didn't ask her to do it!" Charlie snapped. "I didn't want her to do it, and if I could change it—"

"Misplaced guilt, Charlie," Becky repeated firmly, cutting him off. "This isn't about you, darling. She made her choice; all you have to do is respect it and be grateful. I know you. You care about her too much to treat her like this."

"I'm trying to keep her safe," Charlie insisted.

"Then why can't you tell her that, Charles?" Becky replied. "Why won't you talk to her?"

"Because…" Charlie hugged himself and stared at his knees, hunching them closer to his body. "Because I'm quite certain she is much better at talking me into nonsense than I am at talking sense into her." Charlie glared fixedly at his knees. He could feel his sister's expression from across the room. "Stop smiling at me, Becky."

"You're behaving like a child, sweetheart," she warned him affectionately.

"That's my prerogative," he huffed.

"Well, don't be surprised then when everyone else tries to parent you," she retorted.

Charlie looked up from his knees to gaze at her, but her eyes were fixed on her stitching.

"You sound like Michael," he commented.

"That's because he's a smart boy," Rebecca smiled. "Even if he does have unfortunate taste in men." She gave Charlie a sharp look. "Don't tell them I said that."

"Said what?" Charlie responded obediently, knowing very well that Rebecca liked Julian a lot more than she pretended. She smiled and extended the fiction by pretending to ignore him.

Becky tied off her stitching and snipped the thread, smoothing the sleeve of the dress and admiring her work. She made a small noise of approval and then pulled out a new reel of thread, swapping colours and continuing her work.

"You're looking rather scruffy, Charlie," she commented to the dress, her eyes fixed on her sewing. "If you're going out with Florin tonight, you should have your hair cut."

"No," Charlie replied automatically.

"If Susan catches you looking like that, she'll get the scissors herself," Becky warned.

"Oh, I do recall," Charlie huffed. "You remember what a disaster that was last time? Do you really want a repeat of that?"

"I'm not the one who was supposed to learn the lesson from that," she smirked at him, tugging the thread through carefully and setting the stitch with care.

Charlie glared harder.

SHILLING & FLORIN BOOK FOUR

3

Twilight was settling dark and still across the city. The weather was mild and it served as an unpainted canvas for the noise and revelry of the city to splatter. Charlie was nervous on the doorstep. He remembered a time, that felt like it hadn't been so long ago, when he had not been nervous on this doorstep. A time when he had been irritable and impatient, when it had felt as though Pound was wasting his time, and Pound Junior was nothing more than a vulgar nuisance, and Florin had barely been a scratch in his notebook. A time when it had been necessary to all but drag him to the house just to see them.

Now he was here nearly every day, and he was always nervous on the doorstep, and he wanted to blame Harry for the guilt and the stress and the anguish. But that was just a crutch. He wanted to blame Henry for exacerbating all those feelings with his constant reproach. But the reproach wasn't new, which made the excuse all the more pitiful. He wanted to blame Amy. For everything. But nothing was her fault, and he didn't know how to pretend it was. She hadn't done anything but exist. It just so happened that her existence was exquisite and glorious, and poor Charlie had noticed.

He knocked and was admitted in a regular daze of anxiety. No, he did not want anyone to take his coat. No, he did not want any refreshments. No, he was happy to wait in the library like normal. He liked Pound's library. It was a space of reprieve, solitude, and learning. There were always plenty of distractions. Besides, books really tested the edges of his mantras on possession and ownership. He was all for dismantling the class system, restoring power to the people, and redistributing the wealth… but book wealth… well, that was slightly different. Books were knowledge. That was its own kind of wealth… and you measured it differently. Somehow.

People were allowed books.

They were not allowed crooked books. Books could either be in use, whereby strewn upon any available surface was acceptable, provided the book was not being severely damaged; or they were away on the shelf, and thus should be neatly aligned in the appropriate place. Charlie began to straighten a shelf of offending books. A small voice in the back of his head that sounded suspiciously like Rebecca told him these were not his and he shouldn't touch them. He ignored it.

Henry found him first. Lord Pound strode quietly into the doorway, his cane tapping lightly on the ground as he approached, leaning on it for support.

"You've had your hair cut," he commented.

Charlie turned. Pound's arrival had coincided with his completion of the book straightening, but he had clearly been spotted. Henry's expression was a permanent stone mask of weary grief, but right now it was touched at the edges with wry amusement. That was the look he wore when he caught Charlie doing something his Lordship would have described as 'odd but harmless'. He touched his trimmed locks self-consciously, eyeing Pound apprehensively and wondering when the old man's steel grey sideburns had become too big for his face. He worried that the man had shrunk, more than the hair had grown.

"It wasn't my idea," he admitted of the haircut. "Speaking of bad ideas…" His hand dropped from his hair and he began to fidget with his ring. "Are we sure this is a good one?"

"It will be good for Amy," Pound insisted, his voice still as strong as ever, even if his appearance had developed a touch of fragility.

"And I would do anything to help her, Pound, I would…" Charlie trailed off, twisting his ring frantically like he was trying to screw his finger back on. Pound was already giving his impending 'however' a stern look from beneath dense eyebrows. "However," Charlie continued nonetheless, "there is the libel case to consider…"

"If you were really considering it, would you be here with flowers every other day?" Pound interrogated.

Charlie flushed. His voice became small and weak. "That's what you do for people who are recovering…"

"Once, Charles," Pound smiled at him. "You do it once, with a get-well card. You look like you're wooing her."

"I'll stop," Charlie told the carpet with sick

embarrassment.

"I'd rather you didn't," Pound replied. "If you avoid her completely, she'll take matters into her own hands. Your strange behaviour is much easier to defend than hers."

"That's not good enough," Charlie muttered, still facing the carpet. "I have to learn. I have to do better. Just… just explain the situation to her and I'll…" he trailed off, looking between the locked window and the blocked doorway.

"And you'll what?" Pound replied warningly.

Charlie froze like a deer in headlights, still trying to calculate which exit was the better option.

Pound sighed and tapped his cane. "Sometimes I can't tell where your neural divergencies end and your deliberate antagonism begins."

Charlie pursed his lips and frowned. He wasn't entirely sure about that either.

"You're not running out on us, Charles," Pound warned him. "Not tonight. I have the libel case well in hand, so that's not an excuse you can use. The ladies will be down in a moment, and it will be good for Amelia to have an evening out with her friends. You're not ruining this for her."

Charlie stopped and cocked his head, almost echoing the word 'friends' but holding the question back. Sure enough, there were the sounds of multiple women descending the stairs together, talking and laughing. Charlie tipped his head the other way in consideration. That certainly made things easier, although he wasn't usually one for company. The knowledge that it wasn't just him going out with Pound and Florin, that it wasn't some sort of unwarranted intervention, was profoundly comforting.

For all of five seconds.

Then Henry was in the room, and the ladies were in the doorway, and Florin was right there. They all looked at him in a way that made him far less confident that it wasn't an intervention. Amy's friends had the coy expressions of people who knew something about him that he didn't know, which was deeply unsettling. And Amy… Amy looked like she always did. There was a healthy colour back in her warm brown cheeks and her auburn curls were pinned to frame her face. Her green eyes were soft when she looked at him, like she missed him. It was instantly agonising.

"Charlie," she smiled hesitantly when she saw him, "you've had your hair cut."

Charlie made a sound of shy and reluctant acknowledgement. He couldn't meet anyone's eye. They were all staring at him and he wished he had jumped out the window after all. It technically wasn't too late to try.

"It's still getting in your eyes though," Amy commented, moving towards him.

Then she was standing close, and her fingers were trying to smooth his scruffy straw hair from his face, and he could smell her perfume, and he wished that they were alone after all because it was much too hard to have an audience for this.

"How did you get that bruise?" she asked, uncovering the dark smear he'd been hiding at the side of his forehead.

He tried to say 'Jasper' but it came out as another pitiful sound of discomfort. He swallowed the lump in his throat silently, forcing air into his tight lungs and trying again.

"Jasper," he all but whispered the name and messed the hair Amy had been trying to straighten. "Hit me with a thing… it doesn't matter. Susan cut my hair. She ambushed me. Rebecca said I was getting scruffy."

"You're usually scruffy," Amy smiled at him.

Charlie drowned in that smile. Not a sweet, poetic submergence of devotion. An ugly, choking, thrashing of his soul; painful and suffocating and desperate to survive, despite the impossible waves and pressure overwhelming him. She was so beautiful and so patient and so alive. When he looked at her he was flooded with emotion, too deep and overpowering to breathe or speak. The back of his mind was still somewhere else, in memories he could still feel on his hands. The way she had felt in his arms, limp and bloody and dying. The firm, stiff feeling of her corset, rough and soaked with blood. The heavy weight of her body straining against his fingers and going cold. That was so far away from now. But it was right here, still present, because she was.

"Shilling, are you all right?" Laura inquired from across the room. "You've gone rather grey."

"Have you been getting psychiatric help?" Jane added, as though she could see his trauma on his face.

Charlie shook his head, but when he opened his eyes and looked at the room, Florin was all he could see. She was looking at him with understanding and she *knew*. She knew. He couldn't go to a therapist. Even in his circumstances, doctor-patient confidentiality would not cover murder. Amy knew.

"That's what I'm for," she answered her friends, slipping her hand into his and squeezing reassuringly. "But let's get you nice and distracted first, shall we? Laura's very excited to see the Great Livre and the dancing girls, and I'm excited for her excitement."

Charlie almost managed a smile. It was hard to believe he needed this more than Amy, and he didn't want to make it about him. It was supposed to be a recovery present for her. At least one of them was recovering.

The dancing girls did, in fact, prove to be a huge success. Amy herself was partial to acrobats and had been in awe of such psychical prowess since she was a child. As someone who found it hard enough to get herself out of bed in the morning, watching people cartwheel and flip and fly through the air on trapezes was inspiring. The sight left her breathless with excitement and her stitches almost pulled just thinking about it.

However, the real strain to her stitches came from sitting by Laura while a group of rather attractive ladies in large skirts, and otherwise revealing attire, danced for the crowd. That was its own kind of treat. The dancers were enticing enough entertainment on their own, but Amy was prepared to admit that the event was made by her and Jane dissolving into hysterics as Laura became a rather raucous and enthusiastic supporter of the act. She almost wished she'd attended with only the girls. Having Charlie and her father there for the more cabaret acts was fine, but she could feel her father's disapproval of their silliness down the line.

Charlie was less of a wet blanket. Or, at least, he was a different flavour of wet blanket. He sat on her other side and he watched the performances with polite intrigue and fascination. Every now and again he would tilt his head curiously, that cute way he did when he was calculating things. She would catch herself, every so often, looking at him, completely distracted from the show by his solemn grey eyes and crooked nose and lips. She wanted to hold his hand and rest her head against his hair and remind him in no uncertain terms that, no matter what he thought, he wasn't getting away that easily.

But if she tried that, he would almost certainly switch places with Henry, and her father would probably support that because she was the one behaving improperly, and all-in-all it was best just to leave it be. At least for now. If nothing else, Charlie was behaving. He hadn't complained or tried to avoid her all evening. He had taken a seat at her side when she'd asked. It was almost as though they could behave as friends again, the way they had when they had travelled to Paris.

They just had to ignore all the history with Harry

and Kopeck and not even think of mentioning the kiss at the hospital. Not with her father nearby, in any case. Amy wasn't sure if he knew, but she hoped he didn't.

For now, it was much safer to sit back and enjoy the show. It had certainly earnt its place as a deserving distraction, and it wasn't the circus' fault she had so much on her mind.

The next act was the Great Livre, the magician whose famous solo act had recently come to ally with other performers. It was adequately entertaining, although she couldn't help but lament that her medical degree took some of the fun out of it. Having a decent grasp of physics and chemistry really took the magic out of, well, magic. At least Charlie seemed to be having fun reverse engineering all the tricks. Amy felt a small smile tease the corners of her lips as she watched his fingers twitch impatiently and his head tip at each step. He was curious about the mechanics, but he was indifferent to the grandstanding.

Livre asked for a volunteer from the audience. Amy panicked and fought as Laura attempted to volunteer her. Fortunately, they were overlooked for Lady Sterling in the front row, who took only the lightest cajoling with some dramatic cape swirling to coax her onto the stage. The old lady looked bashfully excited to be involved in the show as the Great Livre helped her up and sat her centre stage in a small chair. Amy clapped along with everyone else in support. She watched them go through the motions of the magician comfortingly walking Lady Sterling through the *magic* that was about to make her disappear.

They folded a box up around her to obscure her from view and Livre made a show of grandiose gestures and gibberish. Amy could feel Charlie growing bored at her side. Smoke poured from the cracks around the bottom of the box and Amy felt that was a nice touch. There was a flash and a bang to cover the sound of the trapdoor, and then the box fell open to expose a cloud of smoke and the absence of Lady Sterling.

Amy elbowed Charlie to encourage him to applaud the trick with her, even if they could see how it was done. It was certainly theatrical, and the showmanship warranted appreciation. Charlie rolled his eyes and Amy chuckled at him. He almost smiled. She could see the corner of his lips twitch.

The magician put the box back together to resummon their guest, and when it fell open the returned chair was instead home to a bunch of a red roses. The magician took those aside, insisting they would try again and get it right this time, but required audience participation. Everyone would have to say the magic words with them in order to conjure back Lady Sterling.

Amy tried not to laugh as she could feel Charlie repressing a groan at her side. Livre finished his trick, going through the motions once more, encouraging the audience to participate, and the box fell open with the old lady in the blue dress once more in the chair. She was handed the roses as appreciation for being such a good sport, and the magician helped her down.

That was when Charlie started to take note. Amy felt him tense and lean forward. That made her look harder, and as soon as she knew there was something to look for, she spotted it instantly.

"Oh my…" she murmured.

Charlie heard her and shot a glance back. Their eyes met. He knew she'd seen it too.

"I think your services are required, Doctor," he invited, standing in his seat and slinking down the aisle.

Amy quickly leapt up to follow him. She was immediately aware of her friends and father giving her strange looks. Instinct told her to leave it and just follow Charlie, but that always got them into trouble and she knew the others deserved better.

"Something's fishy," she hissed. "That's not Sterling."

Everyone who heard gave her a strange look, but she didn't stay to witness. She rushed after Charlie and followed him down the stairs. He was striding to the front row. She was aware others were following them now, but it was a small enough and single-file crowd that it hadn't caused a ruckus yet.

"Lady Sterling," Charlie addressed her sharply as she made her way back to her seat. "You're looking a little pale, let's have the doctor have a quick look."

"Oh, no, dear, I feel quite fine," she replied.

All her companions caught on as soon as she spoke. The make-up was good, the outfit was exact, but the voice and mannerisms were all wrong.

"I'm going to insist," Charlie replied, grabbing her.

"Charlie!" Amy yelled, trying to catch him before he did something they'd regret.

"Shilling!" Henry's voice came even louder behind

her as they most definitely began to cause a scene.

The crowd was very aware that a strange and scruffy young man had just run up and assaulted Lady Sterling and were all for calling the police to stop him. Except when he yanked her wig off and exposed the recognisable blonde curls of one of the dancers from earlier, the crowd quickly recoiled in confusion.

Charlie looked up and met the eyes of the Great Livre. Amy watched it happen. It was like watching a rabbit realise it was in the sights of a fox. They both moved at the same time. The magician dashed across the stage, screaming for someone to stop his pursuer as Charlie ran and leapt, clearing the edge. One of the weightlifting strongmen placed himself in front of Livre and braced himself to strike Charlie as soon as he came in reach. Charlie dashed at full speed, leapt, bracing himself, and plunged both feet first through the trapdoor. Its hinges and latch were not designed to accommodate the propelled weight of a full-grown man trying to break through. The strongman looked confused, the magician shoved back past him, looking panicked.

Amy left the embarrassed dancer with her friends and rushed to the stage, bundling her skirts in her hands.

"Florin!" Charlie's voice bellowed up through the trapdoor.

"Charlie! Are you hurt?" she called back, dashing to the hole in the stage and kneeling down to peer through.

The entire circus was in chaos now. Her father was

calling in uniformed officers stationed near the park. The magician had already tangled with one trying to slip out the side and had been hindered by their own crowd. Amy peered into the dark depths under the stage. Small lanterns lit the workspaces for the stagehands and gave enough light for her to make out shapes and shadows. They came into focus, and she saw Charlie holding a candlestick threateningly towards two clowns who held an unconscious, bound, and gagged Lady Sterling in her underwear.

Amy felt a wave of relief and guilt hit her as she promised she would be right down. She wanted to believe that the relief was because they had clearly intervened in time, but the accompanying guilt was all too aware she was intensely relieved that the intervention was warranted. If they had caused this much fuss and ruined the show over a trick, she would have been deeply humiliated.

She motioned to her father and brought him and two uniformed officers with her as she snuck around to the back entrance of the stage. By then, Charlie had managed to talk the clowns into carefully handing over Lady Sterling, whom he was attempting to rouse.

"Here, let me," Amy offered, kneeling down with him and beginning to check her over. "Lady Sterling? It's Doctor Florin. There's been an incident, but you're all right."

The old woman was dazed and mostly unconscious. She seemed to have been gassed — another use for the smoke, perhaps, Amy thought — although it did look as though it would hopefully wear off without side effects. In the background, the officers were taking the clowns for questioning and calling for backup and an ambulance.

Amy shared a look with Charlie. Something about the ordeal made him look particularly grim. She could hazard a few guesses, but was also aware that they had saved the day in time. The shadows around his eyes suggested something darker that she had not yet noticed.

It was some time before she found out why. Her attention, quite rightly, was devoted to the care of Lady Sterling. They found a blanket to wrap her in and keep her warm until the officials arrived, although her clothes and jewellery were recovered from the imposter. Amy, with Jane and Laura, were able to rouse her and care for her until help arrived. Once she was confidant Lady Sterling was in good hands, Amy went looking for Henry and Charlie.

She found them together outside the tent, standing with other officers under a ceiling of umbrellas. Charlie was giving a statement, and a warning.

"— make sure they dig a little deeper on this, Pound," he was muttering. "I'm confident this was not just a kidnapping scheme. I've seen the set up before when I stumbled on a couple of the photos in the past. No one would talk then, but we've got the culprits red-handed this time."

"You heard him," Henry nodded to the officers. "Tear the damn thing down if you have to. There could be blackmail material on more than half a dozen people spread throughout the trailers of this circus."

"And obviously be careful," Shilling muttered. "They're careful with the people they target, we should emulate some of that. There could be plenty of evidence of conspiracy and stalking amongst everything else. This is a long-term operation, not a mugging."

"It can be both," Henry added. "Dismissed."

The crowd dispersed and gave Amy plenty of space to sneak up to join Henry and Charlie. She noticed one of the umbrellas staying with them was held by none other than Commissioner Farthing. The Commissioner did not look pleased to be working with Shilling again, but he didn't look surprised either. He did raise an eyebrow at Amy as she joined them. Before anyone could stop her, she snuck up to Charlie and took his hand.

"Are you all right?" she asked.

He turned to her, confusion plain and head tilted. After this long, it was almost funny the sleuth could solve all these mysteries and still not understand why she was asking. Henry sighed deeply at them.

"A night at the circus…" he shook his head. "I can't take you two anywhere."

"It's hardly our fault, Daddy," Amy protested.

"What?" Farthing scoffed. "That Shilling here can't even take an evening off without uncovering a crime ring?"

"Doctor Florin also noticed the discrepancies, Farthing," Charlie told him. "Even without me, I'm certain the culprits would have been exposed."

Amy did not bother to correct him. She kept her eyes down beneath the dark shadows of the umbrellas, exacerbated by night. She could feel her father's penetrating gaze on the top of her head, boring through her skull, but would not raise her eyes to meet it. She was not in the mood to be reproached. They had done the right thing.

Reality hit her sharply as she felt Charlie jerk away. Her mood had been melancholy and she had let it lean her towards repose in the wake of the evening's excitement. But Shilling snatched Farthing's umbrella and yanked it in front of them as a flash spooked the darkness on the other side. Two more flashes followed. Amy realised with a shock that the paparazzi had arrived. A cluster of journalists were gathered at the edge of the cordon. Voices began to yell at them through the night.

"Lord Pound!" someone shouted, "Is it true the carnies were attacking nobles?!"

"Commissioner, have your officers been outdone by civilian detectives again?!"

"Is that another case solved by Shilling and Florin?!"

Amy felt a light spattering of rain across her face as the umbrella was used to shield them from the press, but she was far more concerned with Charlie's arm around her waist, holding her protectively close behind the barrier.

"Shilling and Florin, how did you know to come here to catch the kidnappers?!"

"Do you have any comments regarding the rumours of your relationship?!"

"Lovebirds, give us a kiss for the front page!"

She could feel him moving away. He forced the

umbrella into her hands before she could grab him.

"Charlie!" she hissed, worried he was in the mood to start something.

Instead, he pulled his coat over his head and dashed away. She tried not to stare after him forlornly, and luckily felt her irritation had won out. At least he wasn't in the mood to fight anyone. It would have been concerningly out of character if he had. Amy sighed and handed the Commissioner back his umbrella. He took it from her with consideration, carefully placing himself so that she was still shielded from the paparazzi.

"Vultures," he bristled in disgust. "I apologise, Lord Pound, Doctor Florin, I know they're vile, but please try and ignore them."

"Easier said than done," Henry grumbled, putting an arm around Amy's shoulders and holding her close.

Amy sighed as she leant against her father's stiff woollen coat. The fabric was coarse against her cheek, and she almost wished they'd opted for another quiet night in. She had to console herself that things could be worse. They had managed to help people tonight, or at least Lady Sterling, if nothing else came out of it. Also, she had managed to spend the evening with Charlie, exchanging real words, even if they were — as Farthing put it — uncovering a crime ring. And he'd only run off after he was spooked by the Press. It was a start.

Then his voice came out of the darkness.

"Amy!" Charlie yelled, hurrying back through the light misty rain.

All three of them startled. Amy shared a look with her father. Charlie never used her first name. Henry's expression told her that he'd caught it too. Something was very wrong. They hurried his direction and met him halfway.

"Charlie, what's wrong?" she asked, huddling under the umbrellas as he joined them again.

Her gaze sought the edge of the cordon he'd come from and she saw a small, dirty face peeking through. One of the kids who fed him information. Charlie dropped his coat back on his shoulders and wiped the thin film of water from his face. She could see the tiny beads of rain, light and sparkly, in the fibres of his coat and through his hair. His eyes were desperate and pained when he looked at her and she knew that expression. She knew what to ask.

"Who?" she demanded, knowing only danger to someone Charlie cared about could make his eyes tighten that way.

"Skipp," he choked.

"Take me to him," she insisted, grabbing Charlie's hand and leading him away before anyone could try and stop them.

4

Charlie had panicked the entire way home. His heart felt tight and strained in his chest, but Amy knew. She understood. She knew Skipp. She knew Charlie and she kept him as calm as possible. It helped to know he was taking the best doctor he knew with him. The panic flared again when they made it to the bakery. Terry met them at the back entrance and led them upstairs. Charlie felt like he was going to puke when he saw all the blood. Mike's siblings were with him, all sitting gathered together on the floor. Harriet was helping him hold a fresh cloth to his face, while Wilber took the old blood-soaked rags away.

Amy began to roll up her sleeves the instant they were in the room, and her business-like manner immediately soothed Charlie's fears.

"Right, let's clear some space, people," she ordered, barging through with her medical bag. "Let me have a look."

The Pence siblings scurried away as Amy joined Mike on the floor and moved the cloth carefully from his cheek to check the wound. She made a sharp hissing sound as she exposed the brutal and jagged cuts down the side of Michael's face. Charlie could tell just by looking that it had been done by a broken bottle. Multiple jagged glass points slashed right down the side of his face.

A quiet and murderous rage stirred in Charlie. Something deep. Something new. But not too new. Something that had awoken before, and now could be woken again. He went cold and still as he watched and waited to see if it would rise to seize control.

"It could be worse," Amy tutted at Michael. "The cuts are nasty, but they're shallow. You've still got all your features. We can clean this up and I'll stitch you back together. You're very brave, I'm sure it hurts terribly, but it looks worse than it is."

"Don't patronise me, Florin..." Michael whispered carefully out the unmauled side of his face.

She met his eye with patient understanding. They shared a barely perceptible nod and Amy opened her bag.

Everyone watched in absolute silence while she stitched him up. No one spoke. No one asked anything. They barely even breathed. The only noises came from Michael and Amy. Every now and again he would hiss and flinch in pain, and she would make soft soothing sounds.

She had finished cleaning and stitching by the time noise sounded downstairs. Doors banged, things crashed. There was yelling. Nearly everyone muttered a few choice oaths as they heard the footsteps on the stairs. Charlie braced himself. He caught Julian as soon as he burst through the door. He didn't think he'd ever seen Swift so stressed, but it was nice to know he wasn't alone in his own feelings.

"Mike!" Julian yelled as soon as he saw him, like he hadn't been screaming his name since he burst through the front door.

Charlie stood between them with a cautionary hand on Julian's chest. Terry stood at his side with a similar hand on his shoulder. Michael had instantly turned away. With his face to the side, he almost looked normal, if bloody and grim. He clearly didn't want Julian to see him right now, but Charlie didn't want to be the one to tell Julian that. Also, it didn't feel fair to Julian.

"Skipp, who did this to you?" Julian demanded.

"Give us some space, please, Julian," Amy requested gently. "I want to finish patching him up before you dive in."

"Who did this?!" Julian bellowed. He immediately began to resist, but Charlie pushed back gently, keeping him away.

"Let her do her thing, Swift," he bid softly. "We need to make sure he's okay first."

"Mikey..." Julian choked, his fury clearly only tempered by heartbreak. Charlie could understand. If it were him, all he would want would be to run to Michael and scoop him up, but the doctor was working and that took priority. Michael still had his face turned away from them as Amy carefully began to bandage the wounds. He grimaced in pain as the first antiseptic layers went down.

"You don't have to be here, Swift," he muttered.

"Are you shittin' me?" Julian scowled, his accent

beginning to crack.

Charlie's hand tightened on Julian's chest again, but his eyes were on Michael and Amy. He couldn't look away. He could see Mike's eyes watering, and not just from the pain. He could see Amy's sympathy, gentle and understanding on her face. If he hadn't been looking, he might have missed the next part. Amy's fingers touched Mike's chin, resting lightly on the undamaged side of his face. The touch was gentle and supportive, but firm.

"You might not want him to see you like this," she whispered so softly it was nearly private, "but it's Julian. He loves you, and it will take divine intervention to keep him from you."

Michael looked like he was trying not to cry and Amy went back to bandaging. Neither of them looked at anyone else. Mike kept his eyes downcast, refusing to meet anyone's glances.

Julian wasn't fighting them anymore, although Charlie wasn't certain if anyone else had heard Amy's whisper. Mostly he felt he'd watched her lips move. It almost felt intrusive. That was when he noticed Terry's knuckles still sitting on Julian's shoulder. Bruised and grazed.

"What happened?" Charlie asked him, deducing the connection.

"Dunno, I missed most of it," Terry answered. "Michael was taking out the trash for us, end of day. Some bastard got him in the alley. Scottish prick. I thumped him and he ran off, Mike was bleeding so much I stayed with him instead of chasing the bugger."

"Scottish prick?" Julian turned to him sharply.

"Barely caught the words," Terry shook his head. "Only the accent."

"He said next time he'd slash my throat…" Michael murmured bleakly.

"Or what?" Charlie demanded. "A threat usually accompanies a demand. What did they want from you, Skipp?"

Michael closed his eyes, almost shaking his head, but holding the action as Amy carefully wrapped his stitches.

"They probably got the wrong person," Harriet pouted. "I told you all those secrets you peddle was gonna get you shanked, Mikey."

"Michael…" Julian began softly. The whole room froze as a twinge of the north crept back into his voice. "What did he look like and what did he say?"

Michael still wouldn't look up. The rest of the Pences were sharing shady glances as they realised there was a side to this none of them knew about. Terry cracked first, but more from sense than tension.

"Big guy, ginger hair, beard — quite scraggly, bowler hat and a battered coat," he reported.

"Terrance!" Michael snapped at him.

"What?" Terry retorted. "We were always gonna tell Sleuth, weren't we? It's more effective than telling the bloody police."

"It's me you don't want to tell," Julian glowered at Michael.

"Can you blame me?" Michael turned to him, exposing the bandages across the cut-up side of his face.

"Tell me you're not going to do something stupid, Swift."

"I'm not gonna do anything stupid, my love," Julian promised. "I'm just gonna find this bastard, cut him open, and very slowly feed him his own intestines."

"We're not feeding anyone anything," Charlie sighed, still holding Julian back. "Skipp, we want to keep you safe. That's all. Please, tell us what happened so that we can work out why and protect you."

"Did he mention a name?" Julian pressed at Mike's continued reluctance. His eyes narrowed as Michael persisted in avoiding his gaze. "Did he mention Rory?"

Everyone was staring at Julian now, except for Amy who kept at her work and Michael who refused to look at him. His lips were pinched and his expression pained.

"You're a bad liar, Michael," Julian murmured affectionately.

Mike caved. His shoulders began to slump and the fight went out of him. He still wouldn't look at them and his eyes lingered on the cloth soaked with his own blood. He swallowed nervously.

"He got me across the face with the bottle..." Mike whispered. "I didn't see him coming. Didn't realise. He... he said... 'Rory has to return what he stole, or the next time I'll slash your throat'. Then Terry showed up. That's it. That's all I know." Finally, he looked up at them and glared through the bandages wrapped around his face. "If you idiots do anything to get yourselves in trouble over this, I will murder you myself."

"Noted," Charlie nodded to him. "No trouble, Skipp. We promise. This guy… he didn't happen to have a scar on his face, did he?"

Now everyone was staring at Charlie. He didn't even blink. People had been staring at him like that his whole life. Everyone gave him strange looks. Even Amy had paused to scrutinise him. Michael's good eye narrowed.

"He had a scar over his left eye… and he stank like ale and sweat and smoke," Michael answered slowly. "Why? Don't tell me you've already cracked the case, Sleuth?"

"Far from it," Charlie replied. "Skipper, do you trust me?"

Michael sighed a deep and reluctant sigh. "Yeah," he admitted. "Yeah, of course I do, Sleuth."

"Then let Amy finish patching you up," he insisted. "We all want to make sure you're okay. That's what matters right now. I'll take Julian to get some air and let you have some space. We'll be back to check on you soon, all right?"

"Get some air?" Skipp echoed, full of suspicion.

"We'll stay if you'd rather," Julian replied instantly.

Charlie nodded. "Of course, Skipp. But you either trust us, or you don't. After what just happened, we're not going to take offence either way. If you want us here, we'll stay."

"Speak for yourself, Sleuth," Julian muttered. "We'll take a little bit of offence."

Michael almost smiled. The corner of his mouth strained at Julian's tone, like he wanted to tease him but just didn't have the energy.

"Amy," Charlie addressed her. The way she looked at him when he said her name nearly struck him silly, but he pulled himself back from the precipice again. He couldn't afford to drown in those eyes right now. "Please, if you can get him patched up and comfortable… if there's anything…"

"I've got a few things I can give him to ease the pain," she replied. "Don't worry, Charlie. I'll take the best care of him I know how. You can poke around the alleyway for clues, just don't get yourself hurt — and watch out for Julian."

He should not have been surprised that she had suspicions about their motives. He didn't even deny it. There was no point. Besides, it was easier than the truth. Instead, he gave her a grateful nod and took Julian with him when he left the room. They moved slowly down the stairs and out the back door. Knowing that this was where it had happened, he couldn't help but take a moment to quickly scour the alleyway from the doorstep.

Julian stood patiently at his shoulder, but Charlie could feel the menacing anger radiating from him. He understood all too well. He could see broken glass glint on the ground, and stepped closer to evaluate what he could in the faint streetlamp light. A partial footprint. Charlie began to size it and calculate. It belonged to Terry. No use. Blood splattered across the wall and the ground. He could see exactly where Michael had been standing and the angle he'd been attacked from the splatter. That aligned with what he knew about the attacker. More importantly, it aligned with what he suspected.

Charlie turned to look at Julian watching him. Julian still stood on the doorstep. The streetlight was bright on his long ebony curls but harsh on his features. His hair hung to his shoulders, casting his face in deeper shadows, exacerbated by the dark ferocity in his eyes. Charlie knew he was waiting. Julian knew Charlie knew more than he'd said. He'd known to ask about the scar. Now Swift was waiting to be let in on the gossip, and then he would act to his moniker.

"Fancy a walk, Swift?" Charlie asked.

"You know, I rather do, Sleuth," Julian agreed, falling in step with him as Charlie strode from the alley.

They were two blocks down before either spoke again. The thin damp air and the cold oppressive darkness kept many people inside tonight. Usual traffic drowned out their footsteps on the cobbles, but the world still felt hushed and tight.

"We're doing what I think we're doing, aren't we?" Julian checked.

"Yes," Charlie answered. "We're getting answers. What was stolen?"

"Find me the bastard who cut up Skipp, and I'll tell you everything else," Julian replied.

Charlie nodded. That was fair. He didn't know how it conveyed in his expression, but he could sense Julian shooting him looks at his side. Swift licked his lips almost nervously before he spoke again.

"I know you're not sleeping right, Charlie..." he muttered.

Charlie shot him a sidelong glare, but knew better than to think a simple glance would deter Julian.

"I know you haven't been sleeping and you ain't been right since Kopeck," Julian insisted. "But, for what it's worth, I'm loving this new side of you."

"You mean the enabling?" Charlie muttered.

"I mean justice," Julian asserted.

Charlie wasn't going to fight him on that. The system was rigged and broken. He'd been grappling with that his whole life. Prison fixed nothing and only enabled the rich to lock up their problems and forget about them. Which, in turn, was a breeding ground for more problems. Charlie believed in education over incarceration.

But when push had come to shove, he had fallen to vigilantism. Worse, murder. From a man who had believed capital punishment was wrong.

He didn't even feel guilty about it.

That had been justice for Esther. Justice for Amy. Justice for all the children Kopeck had sold and tortured and killed across the years. For the little voices that still screamed in Charlie's ears on dark nights as they were buried.

He felt vindicated.

The system had helped with that, brushing over his crimes like they were nothing. He was rich. He had connections. Why not use the system to his advantage?

Why not just go and get justice for Michael?

He led Julian to an old inn he knew. The Dagger & Brooch. Julian was just as obviously familiar with it as they came up the stairs to the front door. The pub was loud and busy with all those who sought shelter from the cold and quiet night. A fire burned in the hearth in the back wall, and crowded tables added to the heat of the room. The noise was expectedly raucous. The light was bright and warm. The smell was heavy and unpleasant.

Ale and sweat and smoke.

Charlie moved through the crowds, weaving carefully between tables as he made his way up to the bar. Julian followed right behind him. There was an enthusiastic drunken atmosphere that Charlie knew from experience could turn nasty quickly, if given a reason. As angry as he was, he didn't want a reason. It comforted him ever so slightly to realise that, even with a sense of rage so blind, he still felt rational enough to know he was seeking justice, not a brawl.

Unfortunately, he wasn't alone.

He was nearly at the bar, hand deep in his pocket, stimming coins he was prepared to barter for information, when a loud voice crowed over the crowd. A heavy, raspy tone with a thick accent.

"The prodigal son returns!" the man bellowed, catching everyone's attention. Julian and Charlie both turned to see a large man with scruffy red hair and beard grinning at them across the room. He leant back in his chair, lifting his mug at them. A shiny, fresh bruise tinged his cheek. His bowler hat rested on the table in front of him. He took a smug swig from his cup and smacked his lips. The bar was starting to go very quiet as he added, "I must'a gotten the right lad this time."

Charlie grabbed Julian by the back of the coat, but that just meant he was slowly dragged closer as Julian stalked towards Michael's attacker.

The bar had fallen completely silent. Charlie knew the man's reputation and employer. That alone was enough to silence any room of drunkards. But it wasn't him people were drawing away from. It was them. It was Julian's expression. Those murderous black eyes. Charlie was still holding onto the back of his coat, but he didn't have to see Swift's face to know what it looked like right now. They stopped on the other side of the table from the man. Charlie could feel his fingers shaking on Julian's coat. The man at the table looked unfazed. He took another drink from his mug, slurping loudly.

"Look, no 'ard feelings, lad. Just hand back what ya stole," he encouraged.

Charlie couldn't stop what happened next. He should have. He should have known, and he should have prepared, but, somehow, he still wasn't prepared for this side of Julian. No one else was either.

Julian ripped himself from Charlie's grip, leaping onto the table. Before anyone could stop him, his boot connected with the man's face. Charlie could hear the man's nose break as it was forced back into his skull. His chair was knocked back and he crashed on the floor. Everyone around them lurched and scrambled back to give them space.

Julian stepped down off the table, planting a solid boot either side of the groaning man on the floor, and looking down on him like he was covered in dogshit.

"Who the fuck do ya think ya are?!" he demanded, his own accent roaring back with force. "Ya think ya can come here, to my city, cut up my man, and think my family will protect ya? That is not how this works."

"Julian!" Charlie yelled at him as he saw his friend snatch a fork from the table and grab the man by the collar. Julian ignored him and Charlie couldn't get to him in time. He couldn't do anything. Horror froze him to the floor, the same way it froze the rest of the crowd in waves, tumbling away from the assault like Moses parting the sea.

"Like mah Da says," Julian began ominously, "an eye for an eye, and one extra just to be sure." He spoke over the man's screams as he stabbed both his eyes out with the fork. The man was shrieking and writhing, clutching his mangled face and struggling to breathe as Julian dropped him back on the floor. "Ya shoulda known better than ta take up work for 'im," he rebuked. "Family business always stays in the family."

When Julian stood and turned, facing the pub with blood on his hands and sadism in his eyes, the whole room looked at him like he was Satan. He barely seemed to notice, shrugging it away like it was nothing.

"Go on then," he encouraged them. "Ya can eat 'im alive now, 'e doesn't have much bite in 'im though."

No one moved until he did. Julian began to walk away and everyone scrambled to give him a wide berth. Everyone except Charlie, who stared on, wild-eyed. Julian reached him, his eyes scrolling up and down Charlie's frozen form, taking it in. He sighed deeply.

"Shilling, turn, walk. We're done here," he ordered,

manually taking him by the shoulders and directing him from the building.

Charlie shuffled in awkward, jerking motions as Julian forced him out. Part of him couldn't believe that had just happened. He had been out seeking answers...

No. He had been out seeking justice.

But not that.

He hadn't meant for that. Part of him knew he should have expected it. Part of him knew bringing Julian meant they were out for revenge. That part of him had decapitated a woman and had no moral ground to stand on. But the other part of him, the part of him that was still Charlie, was horrified by what had just happened.

5

Back in the Pence residence above the bakery, Amy was keeping an eye on Michael. He was dozy from the pain relief, but still processing his trauma quickly. He knew he wasn't okay. No one expected him to be okay. Right now, what he needed was to be bundled up in Julian's loving arms with all the drugs Amy was allowed to give him. Except those dunderheads had vanished into the night. She knew Charlie would poke around — his best friend had been badly hurt, she expected nothing less — but she didn't think they would run off into the night before she'd given the official word on Michael's condition.

Still, she knew from experience how headstrong Charlie was. How intensely he brought that out in others. How badly it had affected her. Julian was even worse. She was surprised they hadn't already set half of London on fire in outrage. She was also surprised when they did return without an angry mob pursuing them.

Amy had Michael settled in bed and resting on all the spare pillows she could find. She sat with him, perched on the edge of his bed, and doing her best to comfort him without making him talk.

Charlie and Julian walked back into the room like a

giant warning flag. The first thing that shocked her was the look on Charlie's face. He looked like he'd been shot. There was a stricken pain and fear around his eyes and his complexion was sickly. Julian looked like the grim reaper stalking behind him. He stood tall and imposing behind the little detective, dark and furious and wreathed in black. As soon as he was close enough, she saw traces of blood on his hands that had been poorly wiped away. He was beelining for the bed, but Amy raised a hand at them.

"Wash up, please, gentlemen, before you come near my patient," she requested.

They both stopped. She'd included Charlie in the mix so that Julian had the option of covering his misdeeds, but the first thing Shilling did was cast his eyes down and touch the corner of his mouth. She watched them turn politely and leave the room. Charlie had been sick. Wherever they'd gone, Julian had ended up with blood on his hands and Charlie had puked. That was... awfully telling.

"You think they got that dirty in the alley?" Michael murmured to her, as they listened to their boys bang about in the nearby washroom.

"I think you know them better than I do," she replied. "And I think you know they weren't in the alley."

The bandages hid his tempered grimace, but Amy knew it was there. Michael was exhausted and troubled. Not even the drugs could disguise the pain and fear in his eyes.

"That idiot's going to get himself arrested..." he

whispered, his voice strained and weak.

Now it was Amy's turn to grimace. She knew what he meant. Charlie had gotten lucky. The person he'd gone after had been so awful that everyone had just been grateful they'd died. No one wanted to look the gift horse in the mouth. Julian might not be so fortunate. While Amy would condemn anyone for doing what that brute had done to Michael, there were systems and processes in place to deal with the situation. Even if they used Charlie's help to track the man down, the police should have been notified of the attack. He should have been arrested and charged. Amy could only imagine what had happened to bloody Julian and so affect Charlie.

When they returned, suitably cleaned up, Charlie had somewhat regained his composure. Although, he still wouldn't meet anyone's eye and he was stimming his ring anxiously. Julian still looked dangerous. Whatever had happened, it hadn't done much to temper his anger. It was only when he reached the bed, Amy standing and moving away to give them space, that Julian finally began to soften at the edges.

Tragedy overcame him and wilted the violence from his expression and stance. He sat in the spot Amy had vacated, lowering himself tentatively. His hand reached out, the tips of his fingers moving to brush at Michael's hair, but Skipp flinched and Julian hesitated.

"How are you feeling?" Julian whispered.

"Like I got cut up with a bottle," Michael muttered. He kept his face turned away and his eyes downcast. "Look, Swift... you... you don't have to be here. You didn't sign up for this—"

"Oh, don't be such a git," Julian huffed, his uncertainty dissolving beneath impatience. He clambered onto the bed properly, hauling Michael into his arms and holding him tightly. Mike barely struggled. He was weak and tired and injured, and resistance was futile. Julian pulled him close, resting his cheek against the top of Michael's head and sliding his fingers through his hair. "I'm not going anywhere, you dunce," he whispered. "Amy would have told me if your brain had gotten cut up too, so don't go trying to pull that nonsense. You think this bullshit doesn't just make me love you more? You don't know me so well after all, Skipp. I didn't ask you to marry me just because you had a pretty face, and I'm never going to change my mind over something like this. Michael, I love you. Nothing could make me love you less, not even if you were cursed into a beast by a witch." He nuzzled his hair affectionately. "I'd wear you like an extra blanket under the sheets…"

"Don't make me laugh, Julian!" Michael clutched the bandages against his face, trying to hold back a chuckle and unable to resist a pained grin. "It hurts."

Julian didn't say anything else, but he snuggled into Michael, kissing his uninjured cheek between the bandages and holding his fiancé to his chest like a scared child. The two of them lay tangled together on the bed and Amy watched their affection softly. There was nothing more she could do tonight, and the best thing would be to let Michael rest. She picked up her bag from by the desk.

"I'll come by tomorrow to check on you," she promised. "But it looks like I'm leaving you in good hands."

"The best," Michael smiled, his eyes closed and his head resting sleepily against Julian. "Thank you, Doctor."

"You're welcome," she smiled at him. When she finally managed to tear her eyes from her patient and his lover, she looked straight for Charlie. He was still loitering by the door, twisting his ring anxiously, his eyes clouded and his expression a mystery. He gave her a nod as their eyes met and walked her politely from the room, holding the door for her and following her down the stairs.

They saw Terry again briefly on their way out and Amy assured him Michael should be fine, but that she would be back to check on him tomorrow. He became slightly flustered when she refused to accept payment, but Charlie silenced that with a look and everyone understood. Michael was his best friend and he would make sure he had anything and everything he needed. Amy was his... well, Amy would make sure that the people Charlie loved received the best medical treatment she could provide, and then they just wouldn't talk about it beyond that.

As they stepped into the night, she was trying to work out how to best phrase her question to avoid being blown off. Instead, Charlie spoke first, and his words surprised her.

"Come across to the house," he invited in a hushed tone, avoiding eye contact.

More than a little intrigued, Amy followed closely at his side as he crossed the road and strode up the stairs to the front door of the Guinea residence. Inside the house things were quiet and dim, as though the residents had indulged themselves in a subdued and lazy evening. Charlie ignored everything as he came through, striding up the stairs without a care, confident the house was safe from Jasper's traps. Amy certainly hoped it was. Although, perhaps if she sprung one, he would finally be ordered to stop.

"Rebecca!" Charlie called through the halls as they made their way up the stairs.

"Living room!" she called back.

Amy wasn't really sure what she was getting herself into, but she was still curious as she followed him through to see his sisters. He had made no effort to announce or warn that he had company. It occurred to Amy as they reached the doorway that such things were probably not of note to someone like Charlie. Privacy and decency were something else entirely to him, and it would not occur to him that perhaps his family would appreciate some notice before he sprung a guest on them.

The living room was well-lit and a small, crackling fire in the hearth kept it stiflingly warm. Susan and Rebecca were already in their nightdresses and robes, snuggled up together on a sofa, each with their own book. Rebecca had her legs tucked over Susan's knees and they both regarded the duo in the doorway with wry amusement.

"Good evening, Charlie, Doctor Florin," Susan

smiled at them slyly. If her expression was mischievous, Rebecca's was worse.

"Sorry to ask," Charlie began, clearly oblivious to everyone else's attitudes, "do we have a carriage that can drive Florin safely home?"

Amy noted with a tinge of disappointment that she was back to 'Florin' again.

"You're not staying, Doctor?" Rebecca teased her.

Amy smiled at them. It was hard not to like Charlie's sisters, even if they were being rude. Besides, it was a cheeky impertinence that rivalled the energy that had attracted her to Charlie's friends, if not Charlie himself. She couldn't feel what she did for him and then pretend she was hung up on good manners.

"Apparently not," she smirked back.

Charlie looked between all of them with exasperated confusion, and she almost felt bad for aggravating him. He hadn't been quite right since he'd heard about Michael's attack, and whatever had happened with Julian had made it worse. He was flustered, and the slow dawning realisation of what they were insinuating made it worse. An angry flush tinged his otherwise still greyed cheeks and he shook his head, running his fingers through his hair and messing it. An irritated huff escaped his lips and he looked ready to bolt and relieve himself of the problem. Amy did not like to think of herself as a problem.

"Charlie, darling, what's wrong?" Rebecca called, her tone placating, reassuring him they were just teasing.

"We've had a rather eventful evening." Amy

answered carefully when she wasn't sure Charlie could. He was still tugging his own hair like he was trying to calm down. It occurred to her as she said it that he could be intensely over-stimulated, and possibly even light teasing was not within his capacity to cope right now. She reached out a careful hand and rested it reassuringly on his shoulder, careful to make sure her touch was light and give him plenty of space.

The joviality had gone out of the room. Rebecca and Susan were sitting forward, abruptly realising something was actually wrong.

"An eventful evening?" Susan echoed.

"Well, we uncovered a suspected crime ring that Charlie thinks might have been kidnapping and/or blackmailing people," Amy began. "Then we found out Michael Pence had been attacked and had to get him medical treatment — he should recover completely, although he might not be quite so pretty as he was. I think Charlie's taking it a little hard, understandably..." She rubbed his shoulder gently and he didn't shy away from it.

"Oh God!" Susan exclaimed, covering her mouth with a hand.

"I thought you two were going to the circus!" Rebecca added, bounding off the couch to embrace her little brother.

"We did that too," Amy admitted, letting Rebecca take Charlie from her and enfold him in her arms. Despite the tinge of jealousy she felt, Amy was glad to see that Charlie was happy to be held by his sister and wasn't trying to push away human contact. Given his neural diversities, it would have been just as probable for him to react the other way.

"You said Michael's going to be all right?" Susan checked.

"The damage is all superficial," Amy assured. "I stitched him up myself. He shouldn't sustain any impairment to his faculties, but there will be scarring and trauma."

"Charlie..." Rebecca sighed carefully, "are you trying to get Florin sent home safely so that you can go dangerously galivanting on your friend's behalf alone?"

He shook his head against her shoulder. Rebecca shared a look with Amy, who grimaced.

"I have a sneaking suspicion that Charlie and Julian did their galivanting while I was stitching up Michael," she murmured.

"Mother Mary have mercy," Susan muttered. "Did Julian kill anyone?"

Charlie shook his head again. Amy just shrugged. They had to trust him on that. She had no idea and she wasn't prepared to ask him in front of his sisters.

Susan stood with a sigh. "I'll ask Ruth to take you home, Doctor. Thank you for bringing our Charlie back without any fresh injuries."

No physical ones anyway, Amy thought to herself, but she just gave a gracious nod and let Susan by. She wasn't sure if she should follow, and at risk of committing her own social blunder opted to stay with Charlie, at least for now. In fact, once he had let Rebecca squeeze him and affectionately ruffle his hair an appropriate length of time, he offered to walk Amy back down himself. They passed Susan on the stairs and she informed Amy that the carriage was ready when she was. Amy gave her thanks and continued down with Charlie, unable to help herself dragging her steps.

Part of her didn't want to go, but it wasn't fair to ask to stay, especially not with the implications Charlie's sisters had just teased him with. She wanted to let him know that it had been nice... nice feeling like things were back to normal between them. Nice getting tangled in the disasters he inevitably stumbled between. It didn't feel appropriate though. She didn't know how to say that without making it sound like she was belittling what he and his friends had gone through.

Still, once they were on the front doorstep, the cool night air easing the tension and the parked carriage outside blocking the street, she couldn't leave without saying something. Anything. She turned to him, pausing on the steps.

"What did happen when you went out with Julian?" she asked.

Charlie shook his head. "You don't want to know," he muttered, eyes down and fingers stimming his coat buttons.

There were a million things she could have done, but only one of them felt honest. Amy reached out, heedless of disaster, and placed her hand on his face, tipping his chin and forcing him to meet her eyes.

"I wouldn't have asked if I didn't want to know," she replied.

Charlie blinked. She knew that was the kind of logic

that resonated with him, that settled him. She also knew that she was touching him because she wanted to, not because it was sensible. She was standing too close, her breath catching tightly in her corset as she resisted the impulse to kiss him again. She wanted to. She wanted so badly to kiss him on the doorstep, but there was already a touch of panic flaring in his eyes, and it wasn't right to keep ambushing him like that.

"Florin..." he muttered reluctantly, "the less you know about it all, the better."

With a deep breath and a conceding nod, she let him have that one. After everything else, if he really didn't want to talk about it, she wouldn't force him to. But she didn't take her hand away and she didn't step back. When she finally moved, it was only to pull in closer. Unable to resist and hoping she could find a compromise, Amy leant in, feeling Charlie freeze in panic, but gently pressing her lips to his cheek as a friend.

"You can't keep me safe by locking me out forever, Charlie," she whispered in his ear.

Maybe he'd never feel the same way she did. Maybe that reciprocation was an illusion and she would grow weary of it. But even if she could never win him over the way she wished she could, he still needed to know she was his friend and she wasn't giving up on him. Perhaps she was like Julian in that regard, persistent and stubborn in her loyalty and affection. She could respect his wishes, should he ever make them clear, but he was going to have to respect that she would look out for him, even if he never loved her quite the way she loved him.

She was fairly certain he was intelligent enough to infer that from her tone, and confident that he had, given the way he still stood, frozen, long after she had made plain that her actions were not as forward as he may have feared. With her argument made, she left him unmoving on the doorstep and stepped away to the carriage.

6

He dreamt of her. Charlie tossed and turned restlessly all night, plagued by fear and stress. That was normal these days, although last night had been worse. He only knew he'd slept because he dreamt of Florin. Of Amy. Of the way she felt in his hands and on his lips. Or the way she might. Even that did nothing to ease the anxiety in his blood. He felt it should, but no. It seemed to make it worse.

The faintest pale tinges of first light were breaking through his curtains when he woke for what felt like the dozenth time. He lay awake in his bed, tangled in the sheets and breathing heavily, as he dwelt on all the things poisoning his mind. His mouth was dry and his mind thick with exhaustion. The endless nightmare of everything that had happened with Kopeck wouldn't leave him alone, and it was igniting residual trauma from the Jack of Hearts.

Charlie didn't understand how people like that could do what they did. He understood that they did, and he could comprehend enough of the psychology behind it to calculate the strange justifications they gave for why. His unusual empathy allowed him to understand the greed and psychopathy and madness that drove them, which helped him calculate their actions and stop them.

But at the core of everything, he could not understand how someone could do what they had done. It was the reverse of him. He could humanise monsters. Monsters dehumanised people.

And he had killed one.

He wanted to feel guilty, but he didn't know how. Logic told him that he had saved multiple lives by committing a single murder. A murder the Crown was already lined up to commit in the name of justice.

And it had felt like justice.

Charlie could still feel the handles of his clay cutter in his hands as he had pulled… Kopeck's throat barely harder to cut through than clay. His mind full of Amy and Esther and the other children he hadn't been able to save from Lubov Kopeck.

Last night, before the circus, Amy's friend Jane had asked him if he'd been receiving psychiatric help. It hadn't occurred to him. He didn't like talking to strangers. He didn't really like talking about himself at all. He'd always had Mike for that. His Skipper. He kept him steady.

But he hadn't told Michael the truth about Kopeck, even though he was certain Mike knew. There were plenty of things in his life he hadn't told Mike about. All the worst things he kept to himself. And lying here, dwelling in the darkness, he was uncomfortably aware that he had not been into his studio since the Kopeck case. He had not thrown clay since his tools had been used to take a life.

Logically, he understood why that was. It was the kind of thing he would talk through with Michael until his head was screwed on properly again. But he'd gone down a road he didn't know how to come back from. A road unlike any other he'd traversed. A road from which there might not be any salvation, whatever that meant.

Also, Mike had been hurt.

That was a fresh pain and fear unlike anything Charlie had known. Michael could have died, and Charlie hadn't been there. He'd been jumped in the alley by his house — targeted. If the man had wanted to, if he'd been slightly off or a little drunker, he could have driven that bottle into Mike's neck instead of his face. It could have been so much worse.

The thought made Charlie want to vomit again, which brought back the other horrible memory of last night. Half a block from the bar, when the extent of the violence had properly set in, along with the full comprehension that his friend had caused it while Charlie stood idly by and let it happen, he had not been able to keep hold of his dinner. Julian had patted his back while he had puked into the gutter. There had been no judgement on Julian's part, which Charlie appreciated. He should have known, should have expected that Julian could do something like that, all things considered. It just wasn't a side of him Charlie had been forced to see before.

Thinking of his friends, daylight finally got the better of him. He hadn't wanted to disturb them too early, but once the noise of the city became a hearty drone out the window, Charlie knew it was time to check on Silver and Pence.

It took him longer to get himself up and ready for the day than he expected. Weariness still slowed his movements and his decisiveness. He stopped by his sisters' room briefly to let them know where he was going. They were awake but had not yet made it out of bed, and he didn't blame them. There was an uncomfortable tension about his visit. He knew it wasn't normal behaviour for him to let them know when he was just popping over the road. They knew it wasn't normal behaviour. Now they were worried about him.

Still, perhaps it would be more concerning if he had been behaving normally after everything that had happened in the past few months. The last year of his life had been trying, to say the least.

Outside the house, the day was fine and the street was busy. Mundane reality was a breath of smog-infested fresh air, and it helped to wake him up after another terrible night. He crossed over to the bakery and snuck in through the side, letting himself in carefully. After the night the Pence family had endured, he didn't want to disturb anyone who wasn't already working. Which, he discovered as he came into the back kitchen, was everyone except Michael. Work did not stop just because tragedy struck.

Charlie didn't blame them, but he didn't want to distract them. He crept up to Michael's room and gave the door a tentative knock. It was only polite. Unlike Julian, he did not want to catch his friends doing something they shouldn't. More importantly, he didn't want to catch them doing anything they should.

When a female voice more familiar than air bid him enter, he nearly had a heart attack. Charlie burst into the room, partially aware that he needn't be bursting, and yet unable to stop himself.

"Amy?!" he blurted, shooting through the doorway.

The shutters and windows were open and the room was bright and clean. Michael was still propped up in bed on his pillows and Amy sat at his side. She had clearly bathed and changed since last night, and she smiled coyly when she saw Charlie standing like an idiot in the doorway. Her medical bag was on the bed beside her, and she was checking Michael's face and changing his bandages.

"Good morning, Charlie," she smiled, turning back to her work. "I hope you slept well. I have to say, I'm a little surprised I beat you here."

She was surprised?! Charlie was stunned. It made a strange amount of sense. If Florin had returned first thing in the morning to check on her patient, then certainly she would have beaten him here. As she had. He just... hadn't expected that. Even if it was completely logical. Now he was still standing in the doorway like an idiot. He didn't seem to be able to stop.

"I know it's only the morning after," Amy commented, filling the silence. "But I have to say, Michael, I'm very pleased with how this is healing up."

"Thank you, Doctor," Michael murmured carefully.

Charlie was being ignored. That was fine. Probably. Michael was the one who needed the attention. But it was Amy's attention, and he'd accidentally called her by her first name again, which he kept doing, and he'd seen her cheeky smirk when he'd done it. She liked it when he did that.

God, he was a bloody fool.

What had Michael called him? An idiot. Well, if the boot fit. He was certainly an idiot for her. Speaking of idiots…

"Where's Julian?" Charlie looked around, finding their friend's absence conspicuous.

"You tell me," Michael muttered.

Charlie turned to stare at him and his focus returned. Mike seemed to realise he'd sparked something, turning his eyes to the wall and steadfastly avoiding Charlie's gaze as Amy worked.

"What's that supposed to mean?" Charlie demanded, recovering from his weakness with Amy and striding over to join them. He shut the door quietly behind him and neared the bed, looming for moment over his friend before carefully adjusting his stance so that he wasn't in Amy's light.

"It means he left," Michael muttered. "And I don't blame him."

"Details, Michael, without the drama, if you please," Charlie huffed tediously at him.

Michael glared at him. Charlie motioned encouragingly at him to spill.

"Come on, Skipp," Charlie sighed. "It's Julian. There's no way he left you like this without swearing to return. Everything you know. Out with it. Starting with his inevitable 'I love you more than fine wine, wait for

me over yonder where morning mist meets dewy fields'
or whatever nonsense."

Amy snorted and Charlie couldn't restrain a shy
smile at having entertained her. Even Michael fought
valiantly against a grin, probably more from his injuries
than anything. A wry grin was certainly twisting one
side of his mouth.

"You know…" he mused carefully. "He's never told
me he loves me more than fine wine."

"You should check that when he gets back," Amy
smirked.

"The nonsense, Skipp," Charlie pressed
exasperatedly. "The nonsense and everything else.
Where did the lunatic go?"

"He didn't say," Michael sighed. "Truly he didn't,
Sleuth. He wouldn't talk about what you two got up to
last night, but I thought you were hunting down my
attacker, until this morning he said he was going to go
and deal to the problem and that he needed to fix it."

Charlie pursed his lips thoughtfully for a moment
while he considered that. Then he shook his head.

"With the nonsense, Skipp," he insisted. "I need it
with the nonsense."

"You know all I know!" Michael defended, raising
his hands in exasperated surrender.

Charlie huffed, pinching the bridge of his nose and
trying to be patient with his still badly injured friend.

"Michael…" Amy began softly. She picked up the
Luckenbooth brooch from his dresser and placed it in
his hand, closing his fingers over it. "Charlie needs to
know what Julian said and if he was behaving

strangely. It's going to help him find him. That's why he needs to hear you say all the things Julian would have said to you, to get a better insight into what he's thinking."

Charlie cocked his head to the side and regarded them both. God, she was brilliant. He hadn't been sure how to explain it to Michael, but Amy saw straight through him and clarified it. It was like having his own personal translator. Mike nodded slowly, clutching the brooch.

"Okay, sure, he was… normal, well, normal for Julian," Mike sighed. "He was still angry though. Stayed angry. He… he told me that… that what happened… that it only made him love me more, but that he had to go and deal with why it happened so that nothing like it ever happens again. So that no one comes after us again. He… he insisted that I wait for him, that he'd come back and love me no matter what, that he'd return as soon as he fixed it. All that, as you say, nonsense. I tried to talk him out of it, but… well, it's Julian."

Charlie settled. Everything about his posture and expression settled at Michael's words, until Amy gave him that shrewd look.

"You know where he is, don't you?" she accused.

Charlie nodded. Before he could say anything else, there was a knock at the door. Michael bade the knocker enter, but they were all surprised to find that it was not another Pence sibling behind the door. Constables Wilson and Bond entered the room, moving surprisingly softly for two bumbling coppers.

"Morning folks," Bond nodded politely at them.

"What are you two doing here?" Charlie demanded.

"Looking for you," Wilson replied, looking him up and down. "Just paid your sisters a visit. Lady Guinea said we could find you here. Got reports that you were witness to an attack last night." He stopped and peered around Shilling to the bed and Michael's rebandaged face. "This the bloke then? You still got your eyes though."

Charlie let out the longest, most irritated sigh he could manage. The entire room gave him a look for it, but he didn't care.

"Why is it," he began painfully, "that every time the police want to annoy me, they send you two?"

"We were actually wondering that ourselves on the way over," Bond replied. "But more like why we always get sent to be the ones to deal with you."

Wilson was still looking around everyone else to Michael sitting in the bed.

"Did you hire Shilling to find the bloke who attacked you in the pub?" he asked.

"You're investigating a case without even having a victim?" Charlie rebuked them.

"We got a pub full of witnesses that said you stood by and watched a bloke mangle some other bloke," Wilson replied. "Not that there's any crime in staying out of a fight, mind you. But while plenty of panicked people were prepared to talk about what they saw, and a rather general consensus of corroboration conveyed that much, both the victim and perp are in the wind. No one's seen a hair of them since. Sounds a bit like one of yours."

Charlie pursed his lips in thought while the room watched him curiously. Bond pulled out a small, tattered notebook and flipped it open.

"Our witnesses were generally sure that you were with the attacker, Shilling," she warned him. "They say you arrived with a man with long dark hair, dressed in black, and that you stood by while he assaulted a Mister Al—"

"—Alistair Pennig," Charlie said the name in tandem with her.

The constables gave him withering looks, and even Amy cocked a curious eyebrow at him. Michael had hidden behind his hands at the description of Julian and didn't look in a hurry to resurface. Wilson gave a gruff sigh.

"What in God's name have you gotten yourself into this time, Shilling?" he grunted.

Charlie contemplated his answer carefully, slowly wetting his lips before speaking.

"Pennig was the man who assaulted my friend here last night," he began delicately. "If you want to make a real case out of this, you're going to need to find Pennig. He was alive when my acquaintance and I left The Dagger & Brooch. If he's missing..." Charlie trailed off.

"Yeah, about that," Bond added, checking the notes, "says here that he stumbled out maybe only ten minutes after you, fought a few other people off."

"Also, all accounts," Wilson chimed in doubtfully, "how's a blind man just disappear?"

"The same way as everyone else," Charlie replied

condescendingly. "He's either in hiding or he's dead. Regardless, he was still alive when we left and we didn't kill him."

"Also says here," Bond continued, "you called the attacker 'Julian'?"

The sound Michael made behind his hands was so small but so telling. At least Charlie could pretend the pain in his friend's voice was related to his injuries. The constables looked to the injured man in the bed, and Charlie was eternally grateful that they didn't decide to press him. They looked back to Charlie.

"We would like a word with this 'Julian'," Bond insisted.

"I'm sure you would," Charlie nodded. "Unfortunately, he's out of town. I can go and get him for you, if you find Pennig and charge him for the attack on Michael."

"Deal," Wilson agreed.

Charlie was very aware of Amy and Michael staring daggers into his back, but they didn't fight him. They knew him too well. Charlie didn't believe in the law nearly enough for it to challenge his loyalty. He wouldn't betray Julian like that, no matter how it looked.

"Before you do that, I have something else for your case," he offered. "Skipp, can I have one of these clean note pages?"

"Help yourself," Mike offered quietly.

Charlie thanked him and moved to the desk, scrabbling through Mike's notes until he found a clean piece of paper and a pencil. Then he began to write.

Everyone watched him and he could sense their growing confusion, possibly even apprehension, as he wrote. And continued to write. And kept writing. The energy watching him had clearly expected a tiny, scrawled note. This was a short essay.

Well, actually, it was a short and informal report. Very informal.

Charlie finished writing, folded the note in quarters, and wrote a name on the front. He walked it across the room and handed it to Bond. She looked down and read the name with a modicum of surprise. Wilson, peering over her shoulder, showed even more, raising a full quizzical eyebrow.

"Before you pursue this case too thoroughly, Constables, give that note to Commissioner Farthing. See if that solves it for you, and…" Charlie paused a moment, wondering if his next request would be seen as too rude, and then remembering that had never stopped him before. "And next time I see you, if you can, let me know exactly what his reaction is."

Bond took the note with a smile and tucked it safely into her notebook. Wilson gave him an agreeable nod.

"Good doing business with you, Shilling," he closed their questioning. "I'd say 'stay outta trouble' but I don't wanna waste my breath."

Bond gave Charlie a look that ruefully agreed with her partner, and the two of them gave their thanks for the cooperation and left.

The room was quiet in their wake. Everyone stayed completely silent, listening to the coppers leave the building and get themselves well out of earshot. Charlie moved as soon as he heard Terry shut the front door. He swept across to the bed, a spring in his step and the energy of a new case sparking life through him.

"Get well, Skipp," he kissed the top of Michael's head. "I promise I will go and find Julian, and hopefully bring him home to you before he gets himself killed."

"Very good," Amy approved, clipping her bag shut and standing up. "Where are we going?"

"Where are we what?" Charlie echoed in confusion.

"Where are we going, Charlie, and what do I pack?" Amy repeated with elaboration, giving him a stern look that did strange things to his insides. She tilted her chin and looked at him coyly from beneath her eyebrows. "You didn't think I was about to let you go alone, did you?"

Her expression sparked something in his brain that reminded him of his dreams of her, and he nearly dove out the window in a panic. A hot flush rose up the back of his neck, prickling the skin beneath his collar, and tightening his lungs.

"You can't," he protested, realising that his voice sounded alarmingly strained. "You... you have to stay here to look after Skipp!"

"Michael is healing just fine, and I can have Laura and Jane check in on him," Amy replied coolly.

Charlie blinked. She was so level-headed. It was like this had been rehearsed. She knew exactly what to say, and all he had in defence were meek little protests.

"Amy, you can't—" he argued, reaching a hand up to ruffle his hair in frustration.

"Charlie," she cut him off confidently, reaching up

and stealing his hand. Her fingers were in his hair. She was standing so close. Michael was still in the bloody room! It was his room! If Amy held him now he didn't have it in him to stop her, and he would melt straight through her fingers. He already knew it.

She kept her distance. All one and a half inches of it. Her fingers were tangled in his, keeping him from all his soothing fidgeting as he gave himself over to disaster. Either he would survive this encounter or he wouldn't. Honestly, if he didn't, that might not be so bad either.

"Charlie," Amy addressed him patiently, holding his hand. "I know you don't want to talk about last night, and neither did Julian, but Michael and I aren't stupid and you can't just shut us out. We know Julian did something awful last night. We know, justifiably or not, that he attacked that man and now the police are looking for him. We also know how traumatised you were after that happened. So please, Charlie, don't make this difficult. I will ask the ladies to look out for Michael, and I will come with you to watch your back."

Logic wasn't even on his side and without it he was helpless. But her stubbornness awakened further considerations... other potential dangers. Other options.

"No..." Charlie pondered, a sudden moment of clarity overcoming him. "No... I'll ask the ladies to look after Michael! Florin, you're a genius!"

His previous emotional turmoil vanished in an instant. He grabbed her by the shoulders and kissed her cheek. Now it was her turn to startle. She balked in surprise at his sudden display of affection, quickly growing bashful. He barely noticed, letting her go and turning back to Michael.

"Skipp, you might be about to hate this next part, but it's for your own good," Charlie announced.

Michael groaned. "Could you stop being a madman, Sleuth? Your scheming will give me an ulcer, on top of everything else."

"You're catching hyperbole from Julian," Charlie warned him, grinning impishly.

Michael glared at him, clearly unimpressed with Charlie's new enthusiasm and any ensuing chaos it stood for. Unfortunately for Michael, Charlie was convinced he was a genius, and was prepared to action his plan by any means necessary. He turned sharply back to Amy and froze.

"Florin," he began breathlessly, before realising that he wasn't sure what to say next. She was looking at him with confusion, although not the displeased kind. Her expression was almost hopeful and the instant he fixed on it he was immediately lost in her eyes. She was going to insist on accompanying him. She already had. Even if, by some miracle, he was able to give her the slip and chase after Julian alone, she was smart enough to track them down — at which point she may kill them both before anyone else got the chance. It was… easier just to accept his fate.

Michael seemed to have discerned the issue and, after a moment of watching them stare at each other, rolled his eyes in exasperation.

"For God's sake, Charles," he scoffed. "Stop being a

complete idiot and take her with you. I need at least one sensible person to rescue my lunatic fiancé."

Charlie nodded. Amy smiled. God, it was the world's most beautiful smile. Even hesitant and demure, it still lit up all her face.

"All right. Yes," he agreed slowly. "Florin, you come with me. We need to talk to Rebecca and get some things sorted. Then, we go and hunt down Julian."

7

It was a surprisingly pleasant day for a train ride. The sun was out and the countryside was lush and green, once they made it far enough out of the city. Charlie had scoured every carriage, hunting out the emptiest one and making sure no one was following them. Given what they were chasing, danger was probable, but that didn't mean it knew they were on the scent yet.

He sat backwards, across from Florin and facing her, watching everywhere they had been disappear behind them. She watched out the window for where they were going, her hands folded over a book on her lap that she had yet to open, staring contemplatively out the window. It was a Dawson & Kropp. For some reason, Charlie expected it to be her own. It wasn't. It did conjure a memory though.

"Julian said the craziest thing yesterday…" Charlie began, not sure why he was bringing it up but hearing the words come out anyway.

"I'm not surprised, given everything," Amy replied.

"No, before all that," Charlie shook his head. "Before their engagement. When he first returned. He said he read your book."

"Why did you tell him it was mine?!" she protested.

"I didn't!" Charlie defended. "I didn't say anything, he just seemed to know. He liked it very much, by the way. Would probably have complimented you himself, had he not been so distracted."

"Well… that's nice," she commented. Charlie could see her blushing. The colour was never particularly evident on her skin, but there was a visual discomfort.

"He… uh… he said he liked your portrayal of me, but I don't think I was in the draft I read…" Charlie muttered, wondering why on earth he was bringing that up.

"What are you talking about? You're not in it," Amy replied.

"Well, that's what I thought," Charlie agreed. "I thought it was a strange thing to say."

"I like Julian, Charlie, but he is a lunatic," Amy muttered, still flushed and hot about the face.

"He is," Charlie agreed wholeheartedly, but with a large dollop of affection.

"And you're certain he went to Edinburgh?" Amy checked, as though they were not already on the train heading north.

"It's the only logical conclusion," Charlie replied, absentmindedly twisting his ring and gazing out the window. He had his legs crossed in front of him and had to focus on not bouncing his foot. It was a common tic, but one he knew drew attention and annoyance from more naturally stationary personalities. "I know who Rory is. I know what Julian's done. I know he was up there just the day before — inevitably getting himself in trouble." Charlie sighed deeply. "He must be beside himself that he got Mike hurt. It'll drive him mad, well, madder than usual."

"He stole from somebody?" Amy deduced.

Charlie gave her a nod. There was no point hiding anything from her. Not at this point. She was helping with the case and keeping her in the dark would only hinder them both.

"Duke Sovereign," he murmured, barely above the train noise, silently tapping the seal on his ring with an agitated fingernail.

Amy stared at him. Proper staring too.

"Duke Sovereign?!" she hissed at him, leaning forward conspiratorially. "*The* Duke Sovereign? Duke Albert Sovereign?!"

"The Queen's cousin, yes," Charlie replied. He pursed his lips thoughtfully. "Surprisingly distant cousin, given the monarchy's inbreeding."

"Charlie!" she hissed at him.

He shrugged at her. It was true and he wasn't taking it back.

Amy shook her head in scathing disbelief, sitting back in her seat with an added mutter of "Julian!" like she could scold him across time and space as well. After a moment's thought, she turned back to Charlie and he could see a glint of warning in her eyes.

"I've met Duke Sovereign before, Charlie," she murmured, looking around cautiously to make sure no one was going hear them. "He's a madman. Properly mad. The things he gets away with because he's royalty would make your blood curdle."

"You mean like paying Pennig to come to London

and cut up Michael to get back at Julian?" Charlie replied, cocking an eyebrow at her. "Or did you mean the vast array of people he's cut up with his own hands over the years?"

Amy settled back again, but the warning look in her eyes was growing in intensity. Given her reaction, he almost wished he'd told her everything before they'd left. He might have been able to convince her to stay, given the danger they were hurtling towards. Charlie rebuked himself internally. He was fooling himself if he thought there was any truth in that. The more danger he threw himself towards, the more likely Amy would follow. If he was honest, he liked having her with him. She was possibly the best company of anyone he'd ever met.

Those feelings were reinforced as he watched a sudden revelation dawn in her eyes. The notion budded with shock and blossomed into alarm. Charlie smiled at her. It was probably a little smug, but he couldn't help himself.

"There you go," he smirked. "Good job, Florin."

She stared at him sharply.

"Did you know?" she demanded.

"Of course," he smiled.

"Does Mike know?" she asked, her voice filled with quiet dread.

Charlie gave a slight nod. Amy settled slightly, but her eyes were still a touch wild with revelation and she kept glancing to meet his gaze.

"How long have you known?" she asked.

Charlie's grin tipped even more lopsided than usual.

His expression answered for him. Please, did she really need to ask? Florin rolled her eyes at him.

"Bastard," she muttered.

He chuckled. "My parents were married, thank you, but I'll take that as a compliment."

"And the note you wrote to Farthing?" she continued, following the trail rapidly.

"Told him everything," Charlie grinned. "Even embellished a little."

Amy nearly smiled. "No wonder you asked those coppers to tell you how he reacts."

"I anticipate hearing the cries of his colourful language echo across the countryside as we travel," Charlie smirked.

"How are you enjoying this?" she inquired dubiously.

"I'm not," he answered.

"Then why the big grin?" she asked.

"I love how smart you are," he smiled, acknowledging what had brought the joy on in the first place. Not the situation, which was a disaster any way they looked at it, but the fact that she had deduced so much of it herself.

The warm glow bloomed across Amy's brown cheeks again, beneath her freckles, and the impertinence with which she had been questioning him dried up. It was not dissimilar to the demure smile she had worn when he had agreed to let her join him on this case. With one last shy glance, she opened her book and turned her attention away. He left her to read, stimming his ring as he looked to the window and watched the world pass them by.

Night had fallen by the time they reached Edinburgh. Amy had finished one book on the train and been forced to start another. She wasn't sure she trusted herself to hold a conversation with Charlie right now unless he started it. Otherwise she risked saying something she shouldn't. She risked spooking him off again, especially after she only just seemed to have won him back over. At least he was letting her help with this new disaster. Although, now that she knew more about the situation, she wasn't quite sure how to fix it.

They took their bags and left the train. Rebecca had organised their tickets and called to make all the arrangements for them. Amy wasn't wholly surprised to find a driver waiting for them with a plaque that read 'Mister Guinea'. Shilling wasn't all that uncommon a name, but it wasn't a revelation to find that for the purposes of what they were doing he wasn't using it. Or, at least, Rebecca was making things easier by booking everything under her married name.

The driver helped them load their things into the carriage and Charlie told him to take them straight to the Sovereign Estate. He got a confused look in return.

"I 'ave you booked in for the night at The Shepherd's Arms," he replied.

"I'm sure you do," Charlie agreed. "But we need to get out to the Sovereign Estate. It takes priority."

Their driver looked like he was prepared to argue further, but seemed to think better of trying to take on Charlie's determination. He shrugged it away in agreement. A longer trip meant a higher fare. No reason not to, as long as he wasn't the one getting shot at.

Amy sat in the back of the carriage with Charlie, wishing she could hold his hand and instead simply watching in the dim occasional streetlight as he fidgeted with a ferocious anxiety. It only served to aggravate her own feelings, but she couldn't look away. Her stomach was tying itself in knots. She hoped Julian was okay. She hoped that wasn't a vain hope.

She tried not to think about what it would do to Charlie and Michael if he wasn't. Except she couldn't help but wonder what Charlie would do if he wasn't. As long as she had known him, he had been a wild card. The last time someone had threatened Charlie's loved ones, they had ended up headless at the feet of Justice. She truly couldn't begin to guess what he would do to a Duke if he found out something had happened to Julian.

The trip to the Estate was dark and tense, but as they pulled up at the gate, Amy swore the feelings only got worse. It did not help that the guard who stepped out of the small guardhouse to meet them looked like he could snap the both of them over his knee and throw their broken meat to the dogs. He loomed over the carriage, his scraggy beard filling the window and his breath reeking of old meat and ale.

"We're here to see Rory Sovereign," Charlie told him without the slightest trace of intimidation.

The guard looked them over. He grunted.

"Come back tomorruh," he told them.

"My name is Shilling. This is Doctor Florin. It's urgent," Charlie insisted.

An entertained spark flared in the guard's eyes.

"The Shilling an' Florin?" he leant on the window frame and eyed them up. "Now you mention it, I do recognise ya, lass. Papers don't do ya justice."

"We need to see Rory," Charlie insisted.

"Tough," the guard replied, turning to spit on the ground. "Master Sovereign's indisposed this evening. You'll 'ave to come back tomorruh."

Amy watched as Charlie tried to outstare the guard. There was no point. The only way they were getting in tonight was if Charlie broke in, at which point the odds of getting shot or mauled were not in their favour. She could almost see Charlie trying to calculate if it was worth the risk. Eventually, the darkness behind his eyes settled, as though somehow convinced that Julian would survive the night.

"First thing then," Charlie muttered.

"If it please ya," the guard grinned. "Be seeing ya then."

With a painful reluctance, Charlie instructed their driver to take them away to the inn Rebecca had booked. Seeking asylum under Sovereign's roof wasn't worth it, not even as a means to get in to see Julian that night. As torn as she felt, Amy was grateful Charlie hadn't tried that method.

Besides, it had been a long day already, and she could do with a decent night's rest before they faced off with Duke Sovereign.

Unfortunately, the day wasn't done with surprises. The initial ones were all pleasant as they pulled up to a cosy-looking tavern with a carved ram's head above the lintel. Inside, the inn was warm and well-kept. Exactly the kind of place Amy could imagine Rebecca and Susan staying on a visit. It was a welcome relief from everything else, until Charlie tried to check in and was given only one key.

"I think there's been a mistake," he began. "There should be two rooms."

"No mistake, Sir," the lady at the desk told him. "One room under 'Guinea', Sir."

"Then we'll need to book a second," Charlie sighed, patting his pockets.

"Begging your pardon, Sir, there aren't any free rooms," she apologised. "They're all fully booked."

"Then we have to go somewhere else," he muttered, looking about.

"The Fair's on this week, Sir," she told him sympathetically. "Good luck."

"Charlie," Amy stilled him with a motion of her hand and shook her head. She was too tired to run all over town and they could survive a twin room without scandal — provided Lionel Tanner hadn't followed them to Scotland. "It will be fine. We can cope."

She had truly believed that when she'd said it. She'd continued to believe it all the way up the stairs, and had only begun to doubt it when Charlie had opened the door and they had discovered that it was not a twin room. Rebecca, unsurprisingly, had a sense of humour.

Charlie did not. Charlie looked like he was going to stab someone and it was all Amy could do to keep from laughing. She was exhausted and did not have the patience to take the games between the Shilling siblings seriously.

"I'm going to kill her," Charlie whispered, standing in the doorway. "With my bare hands. I'm going to push her out her bedroom window."

"Oh, give it up," Amy sighed, amusement winning out as she hauled her bag through the doorway and placed it on the left side of the bed, claiming it as her own.

"I'm going to cast her into the back garden from the fourth floor," Charlie muttered, still unmoving in the doorway. "Right onto the back steps, and I'm going to make it look like she tripped."

"You'll be past violence by the time we get back to London," Amy chuckled, opening her travel bag and starting to dig through her things. "Besides, there's an extra blanket here. I can roll it up like a barrier down the middle of the bed for you. Now, come in, Charlie, you're letting the warmth out."

"I can't shut the door!" Charlie exclaimed. "What about the libel case?!"

"Oh for—" Amy stopped herself cursing sharply and took a deep breath. She paused for a moment and began again slowly. "Charlie, no one up here knows or cares who we are. No one is following us around sniffing for anything. I'm not going to lose sleep in a cold and unsecured room just because you're paranoid."

With a sullen reluctance she realised was annoyingly typical of him, he edged into the room and shut the door, loitering by the wall. Amy sighed to herself again as she gathered her nightdress from her bag and tossed it over the nearby folding screen.

Despite the dilemma of the solitary double bed, it was a nice room — warm, clean, and spacious. There was a small fireplace and comfortable-looking armchairs. There were two sizable dressers, a writing desk, and each side of the bed had a bedside table with a bright lamp on it illuminating the room. Even the bed was sizeable and well-padded. It would be easy enough for them to avoid each other. If it turned out to be the honeymoon suite, Amy would applaud Rebecca for such an excellent practical joke. Then probably help Charlie hang his sister out the window by her ankles until she apologised.

It was only once she was safely behind the folding screen, taking a leisurely time to change and ready herself for bed, that it occurred to her what Rebecca had actually done. She blushed so hot and so fiercely she wished Charlie had insisted on leaving the door open. Certainly the room needn't be quite this warm. Eventually, sense overcame embarrassment, and once she'd composed herself, she came back out into the room.

Charlie had made it out from by the wall, which was encouraging. He'd even changed clothes himself, stashing all his belongings by the chairs near the fire. Amy recognised what looked like his baggy pottery trousers beneath a long nightshirt. He was in the process of building a small nest of pillow and blanket on the floor. She laughed when she saw it. He looked up at her, stubborn as a mule, and glared with hard grey eyes behind his scruffy straw hair.

Her heart ached when she looked at him and she decided Rebecca's joke had, in fact, been rather cruel. Amy was certain Rebecca hadn't meant it to be, but it was. It was cruel to make her look at him like this, and stare not just at the physical distance between them, but the endless distance between what they had and what she wanted. Seeing it like that birthed a soft and silent grief in her, and the grief made everything easier. She was familiar with grief.

"Charlie," she said patiently. "I don't want to make you uncomfortable, but I don't want you to catch a cold sleeping on the floor either. It's a large bed, there is plenty of space, and I'm sure the two of us can behave respectably for one night."

"It's not appropriate," he grumbled.

"Why?" she sighed impatiently. "Because I'm a woman? I really think that's a tired excuse, don't you?"

He didn't reply. She shook her head at him.

"If I can share my bed with a murderer, you can share your bed with a woman, Charlie," she muttered.

He blinked. That had gotten his attention. Amy folded back the sheets on her side of the bed before she realised he still wasn't moving.

"I can also still roll up the barrier blanket, if you'd like," she offered.

"I do not need a barrier blanket," Charlie huffed from the floor. "I'm not a child."

Amy gave him a look that suggested his behaviour did not always corroborate that statement and climbed into bed. She made herself comfortable, perhaps hugging the side of the bed a little too closely, and blew out the lamp beside her pillow.

She was almost surprised, but mostly pleased, when she heard and felt Charlie clamber in the other side half a minute after her, seemingly returning both the pillow and blanket he had dragged away. The other lamp went out. They both lay back-to-back, facing away from each other in the mostly dark of the room. The fire burnt low in the grate and was covered by a guard that further dimmed its light. She could feel herself holding her body tense in the bed and was certain he was doing the same.

"I'm going to kill her…" Charlie whispered into the night.

Amy began to laugh. She couldn't help herself. She buried her face in her pillow to muffle the sound while she got herself under control. Charlie gave a huff behind her.

"Really?" he muttered.

"All I ask," Amy sighed, regaining her composure, "is that you don't kick me in the night when you dream about beating up Rebecca."

He promised nothing and she couldn't make out any words in his soft grumbling. At least it added some much-needed levity to the situation. Amy snuggled back into the bed and tried to relax. After a moment, Charlie spoke again, but this time his words just confused her.

"Why don't you care?" he whispered.

"What?" she muttered, rolling over to face him.

He was already facing her. Amy froze when she came face-to-face with him, but he wasn't looking at her. He was staring down and his eyes were half closed. His expression was grim and torn.

"Why don't you care that I… that I killed someone?" he whispered. "You said it… I'm a murderer. You said it like it was nothing. How can you shrug that away?"

Amy sighed deeply and snuggled down again, facing him. Her eyes traced the pale outlines of his crooked face, heavy with regret. With tentative fingers, she pushed a stray lock of hair from his brow. He didn't flinch. She hadn't realised she'd been expecting it until it didn't happen. He stayed completely still and didn't move, but she could hear his breath tremble against his pillow.

"Because I know why you did it," she whispered. "Because I understand. Because I can appreciate that at that time, in those circumstances, it was a lesser evil, and because I know that it tears you up inside."

"No…" Charlie muttered into the sheets. "No, it doesn't. Amy… I… I don't feel guilty. I keep waiting for it. I keep waiting to feel guilty… but… but mostly I just feel guilty about not feeling guilty…"

"How terribly English of you," she chuckled.

"I'm serious," he insisted. "I took a life! The worst sin, the first commandment, Amy, I took a life and I don't even feel bad about it."

"Yes, you do, Charlie," she whispered softly. Her eyes sought his and he finally looked up at her. Even in the half-existent firelight, his grey eyes were like pools of moonlight, though fraught with confusion and dread. She knew, looking at him then, that it was the first time he had properly admitted what he'd done out loud to anyone. He was terrified of the action and of his own uncertainty and confusion.

And they were being silly. They were both being utterly ridiculous. She couldn't believe it had taken him confessing his crime to put that in perspective. With a deep sigh, she put a comforting arm around him and snuggled into him, feeling the warmth of his body against hers.

"You do feel bad, Charlie," she whispered. "You wouldn't be so caught up on it if you didn't. No one who knows you, not even the people who know what you did, are worried you're about to turn into a serial-killing psychopath. You didn't do it for pleasure, you did it because your hand was forced. You killed to save lives, and that makes it self-defence. I didn't mean to trigger you with my comment, and I'm sorry, but I couldn't have done it if you weren't carrying guilt."

"I think I mostly feel confused…" he admitted.

She didn't push and waited until he felt comfortable to talk. He shifted slightly beneath her arm and it was the first time she felt him stir against her. With their faces close and the blankets piled over them, it almost felt as though they were in their own private world, sheltered from reality by the dark cloak of night. Here, they could say anything, even talk about the things no one should speak of, and she wanted to hear whatever he'd been hiding from the daylight.

"I used to believe that killing someone was the ultimate evil," Charlie whispered to her. "I listened to everything my father had to teach and I believed that lives were God's alone to take. After he passed, that was the only part I never doubted." He paused, his voice growing thick. Amy moved her arm back, placing her hand to his face and tracing his cheek with the side of her thumb. "But when I saw her…" Charlie continued sickly. "When I saw little Esther hanging there… Kopeck tortured and murdered a little girl for fun. It wasn't to get my attention. There are millions of ways to do that. She chose to do it because she wanted to. At worst it was to provoke me, and it worked. I fell for it. I killed her and it was easy." Charlie let out a long and trembling breath, like he was finally relieving himself of something terrible and heavy. Amy felt it shiver across her throat, tickling the skin above the collar of her nightdress. He shuddered beneath her hand. "It was easy, Amy. It felt just. It felt righteous. No matter how many ways I look at it in my head, I can't see the action as wrong, and that scares me. Was I wrong or was I inevitable? Was I simply God's instrument of hubris?"

"The fact that these questions haunt you tells me you're going to be okay," she replied, tracing his cheekbone again soothingly.

"I am unaccustomed to settling for 'okay'," he breathed.

Amy laughed quietly and was pleased when his own chuckle joined hers. At least he knew when he was being foolish. Sometimes.

"Amy…?" he whispered curiously to the pillows.

"Yes, Charlie?" she replied.

"Why did you kiss me at the hospital?" he asked.

"Because I wanted to," she answered simply, knowing the answer was for herself as much as it was for him. In this safe dark, where he was spilling his soul like ink into water, there seemed no logical reason not to join him. He didn't even flinch from her answer.

"But why?" he insisted, as though genuinely confused.

She gave a small breath of laughter, like that wasn't abundantly plain, especially to one supposedly as clever as him. But if he really didn't understand, then he was going to have to endure the explanation.

"Because…" she began extremely slowly, "I think, rather unfortunately for both of us, I'm very much in love with you, and while I was hospitalised, and you were trying to abandon me, I was on enough drugs to sufficiently lower my inhibitions. I kissed you, Charlie, because I wanted to, because I'd wanted to for a very long time, and there simply wasn't enough common sense in the room to stop me."

"How's your common sense right now?" he breathed.

"Appalling," she replied.

"Good." His response was half lost in his hand on her cheek and his lips against hers. It wasn't like the kiss in the hospital. It wasn't even like the kiss in the drawing room, although that bore more similarities. This time they both knew exactly what they were doing and neither of them were fighting it. She pulled him into the kiss, sliding her fingers through his hair. He rolled closer, pressing his body to hers beneath the blankets. They kissed like somehow it was the first time and the hundredth time all at once, like they knew each other intimately and had for years, but hadn't dared step across this threshold before.

Charlie paused. He pulled his lips away and tilted his head, listening.

"What's wrong?" Amy gasped, still holding him close.

"It's too quiet," he murmured. "There are definitely spare rooms available."

"Well, it's a bit late to investigate that now," she laughed, dragging him back to her.

He didn't resist. His mouth found hers again at the same time his hands found the bow at the front of her nightdress and began to carefully unlace it. The neckline came loose and his fingers traced under the edges of the fabric, slowly pushing it down across her shoulders.

She grabbed his nightshirt and coaxed it up, until he raised his body to let her tug it over his head. She cast it onto the floor and ran her hands up his chest, pinning him to the mattress as he started to kiss down her throat. His lips and breath were hot on her skin, but his hands were cool as they began to investigate down the open bodice of her nightdress.

Every sound she made was involuntary. Every breath an unwilling, flustered gasp. She could feel a hot sweat prickling across her skin, compounded by a burning flush everywhere they touched. His mouth was wet against her collarbone. His hands firm and sure against her breasts. She could feel a longing urgency in his touch that mirrored her own.

She tangled her fingers in his hair again, letting the soft strands slip through her grasp as she clutched him to her. His lips travelled ever lower and she traced her hands back down across his body before he escaped her touch. His chest was strong and muscular. She remembered the pottery studio and the surprise she had felt when she had seen what hid behind his battered clothes and wiry frame. It was as much fun to peruse with her hands as it had been with her eyes.

His arms were strong and steady as he continued to lower her nightdress, letting his lips trace across her bare breasts like he was teasing her skin with the promise of a kiss. She moved to straddle him, pressing herself over him as though urging him on. She wanted his hands on her, to feel him touch her everywhere at once. She brought her mouth back to his and he delivered on the promise, kissing her so passionately she knew she was gasping his name.

It wasn't enough. None of it was enough. She couldn't believe she'd wanted him for so long and wasted so much time when everyone else had known. Lizzie had known. Lizzie had touched her like this knowing the whole time that it was Charlie that Amy really wanted. She dragged her mouth across his skin, tasting the sweat beading his neck. His hand clutched at her thigh as she drew her teeth gently down his body, resisting the urge to devour him. One curious hand slid further and she reached down, fumbling around the front of his trousers. She could hear him panting near her ear as she brought her kiss back to the edge of his jaw.

"Amy…" His voice trembled in panic.

She kissed him harder. Touched him harder, forcing the intensity she felt into every part of her body and every inch that connected with him. He grabbed her roughly and tossed her back onto the mattress. She loved it until the moment she felt the coldness of his absence.

"Charlie…?" she opened her eyes in confusion, looking around wildly.

She was alone in the bed.

"Charlie?!" She followed the drag of the blankets across his side and peered over.

He was curled up on the floor, his nightshirt pulled over him. She could see him shivering and twitching, could hear the panicked labour of his hyperventilating.

"Don't touch me!" he gasped.

Amy sat in the nest of tangled blankets and looked down on him. She carefully pulled her nightdress over her bare chest and held it in place, watching with patience and concern.

"I won't," she promised softly, feeling her heart sink. "You're safe, Charlie. I won't touch you."

He was still shivering and gasping under the shirt. She wanted to comfort him and rub his back while he endured the panic attack, but knew she had to respect his wishes, especially given what had seemingly set him off. She couldn't tell if he was crying or just panting, and she wasn't going to pressure him to find out. Instead, she took her own deep and slow breaths as she reluctantly put her nightdress back on properly and tied it shut. Her racing heart was beginning to slow, but she wasn't sure she was pleased about it.

She sat and waited until Charlie's breathing steadied. He still didn't move, staying fixed in the foetal position beneath the makeshift blanket of nightshirt. Amy wasn't sure if she should say something. While she was trying to decide, Charlie spoke.

"I'm sorry," he whispered heartbrokenly, his voice decidedly tearful.

"It's okay," she replied, not feeling completely like it was but with no other idea what to say. "It's okay, Charlie. You… you can come back to bed. I won't touch you."

She saw movement beneath the shirt, a frantic shaking of his head.

"You can't stay down there, Charlie," she negotiated patiently. "You'll freeze."

"I'm sorry…" he whispered it even more weakly than the first time.

Amy watched him several moments more. The longer she watched the more painful it felt. Apparently, there were still things she didn't know about him after all.

"Charlie," she began again in her gentlest clinical voice. "I'm going to roll this blanket up and put it down the middle of the bed. I won't cross it. When you're ready, you can get back in your side and I promise I won't touch you."

She didn't put any questions on him and she didn't leave space for discussion. She did exactly what she said she would and lay down again on her side of the bed, hugging the edge, just as she had when she had first climbed into bed. The silence of the room was pained and neither of them moved. Amy lay awake for what felt like a very long time, possibly an hour, before she heard him move. She listened to all the soft sounds of him pulling his shirt back on and climbing ever so carefully into the bed behind her.

At least once he was safely back in the blankets she felt herself relax slightly. He wasn't going to catch a chill or a cramp on the floor. Still, it was a very long time before either of them was relaxed enough to actually get any sleep.

8

Daylight brought no reprieve from the awkward tension. Both of them rose and dressed tentatively at dawn after an uncomfortable night. The entire way from the room, through breakfast, and back into the carriage, they never made eye contact. They couldn't even communicate in whole sentences. Everything was polite, distant, and as short as it could be while still maintaining basic civility. Amy didn't know how to ask, and Charlie didn't know how to tell.

The most Charlie had spoken to anyone was to check with the front desk how long the room was booked for. Rebecca had reserved it for the week. Charlie had insisted they wouldn't need it for that long, but it was a convenient space to leave their belongings — save Amy's medical bag, which she decided to bring with her. Better safe than sorry, given what they were about to do.

The carriage took them back to the Sovereign Estate, winding out of the city and around the hills to the expansive property, with its high stone walls and wrought iron fences. The same guard from the night before met them at the gate again with a gap-toothed grin.

"Aye, the return of the sleuths," he smirked. "Ya welcome to try ya luck at the house now, if ya feelin' brave."

"Trust me, we've dealt with worse," Charlie sighed.

"I'm sure ya 'ave," he grinned. "Speakin' of — ya wouldn't mind signin' this for me before I get the gate for ya?"

Both of them felt the cold pull of dread as the guard produced a battered piece of folded newspaper. Charlie assumed it would be something from the Jack's case. Amy thought something more recent, perhaps even the circus.

Lionel's fictional masterpiece about their elopement to Paris was thrust under their noses.

It was like getting shot by a highwayman.

Charlie took it first and quickly scrawled 'We did not elope. We were working' above his name and pointedly obscured half of Lionel's story. Amy followed with her own signature and a postscript of 'We were pursuing a French thief'. The guard took it back, and he did not look troubled about Charlie defacing his article. He gave an amused snort.

"Well, I'll be," he chuckled. "All right, get on with ya then. Shilling and Florin… see if ya can solve the case of the Sovereign family!"

He hauled the gate open and the carriage drove them through the high stone archway and up the long gravel drive. The family home of this particular branch of the Sovereigns looked like a cross between a castle and a mansion, or a castle that someone had renovated for comfort, which was more likely. The grand entrance and massive front doors should have been intimidating, but neither Shilling nor Florin were in the mood to be intimidated. They strode out and knocked like they were working as reclaimers, and were met at the door by a surprised butler.

"Shilling and Florin," Charlie introduced them brusquely.

"*The* Shilling and Florin," Amy added, noting the man's surprise and deciding to take advantage of the same enthusiasm they had been shown at the gate.

"We're here to see Rory Sovereign," Charlie finished.

The butler looked at them carefully, like a man with a consistently interesting job that was about to get more interesting. He eyeballed the state of them, their expressions, and Amy's medical bag.

"Right this way," he invited, like any dispute of the issue was above his paygrade.

They walked in silence as they were led into the castle and up several floors. The butler did not knock when they reached their destination, but opened the door on a lavish bedchamber without so much as an introduction. The best he could do was a deliberate look from under severe brows that seemed to say, 'good luck'.

Charlie wasted no time and barged straight in. Amy shared a rueful look and grateful smile with the butler before following Charlie. The chamber was very much befitting of royalty, with a view that could nearly see all the way back to Edinburgh, if not for the factory smog. The four-poster bed was big enough for a small family, but only one slumped figure sat, half-dressed, on its edge.

"Hello Rory," Amy greeted him sympathetically.

Julian looked up at them, tossing his hair back from his face and exposing the large, shiny, dark purple bruise that took up half of one of his cheeks. He glared like he was going to stab someone.

"I told Sleuth that if he ever called me that, I'd break all his fingers," Julian warned. "Ya get the one pass, and then don't think I wouldn't, Doc."

"Julian…" Charlie groaned, kneading his forehead. "Do you ever get that little voice, that little voice in the back of your head, that tells you not to do something? That warns you when what you're about to do is a bad idea?"

"Ya mean Michael?" Julian replied. "That's why I didn't tell 'im about any o' this."

Amy and Charlie nearly shared a look. They glanced at each other, their resignation over Julian's incompetence almost winning out over their own discomfort, and then quickly looked away again. Amy's eyes immediately returned to Julian and his condition.

"Do you want me to take a look at your injuries?" she asked, spotting more bruising that suggested the possibility of cracked ribs.

"I want you two to tell me what ya doing here," he spat. "Ya supposed to be protecting Mike!"

"Don't worry, Swift," Charlie assured him. "He's safe. I promise. We wouldn't be here if I wasn't confident that Skipp was secure."

Julian almost settled, but there were emotional storm clouds about him blacker than pitch. The anger, resentment, and bitterness nearly oozed from his pores. He still had that homicidal look in his eyes he'd had since he'd seen Michael bleeding on the floor. It disappeared for a moment as he rubbed the exhaustion from his face with both hands, ignoring the pain from his cheek. There was a shiver of tears in his sigh, but no sign of them in his appearance.

"He said he'll kill him…" Julian whispered. "He said if I don' get it back, he'll kill Mike. But I don' know where it is—"

"I can get the painting back," Charlie announced. "The Platine? You fenced it through Elizabeth Denarius?"

Julian and Amy both stared at him. Charlie was stimming his buttons, but otherwise remained unfazed, meeting Julian's eye a little, if only for confirmation, and ignoring Amy completely.

"I didn't know ya were keepin' such a close eye on me, Sleuth…" Julian muttered.

"You also knew about Pennig — who the man who attacked Michael was," Amy recalled.

Charlie breathed deeply. "I knew Pennig did regular work for Sovereign. I kept an eye on him anytime he came to town, just in case. Had an ear to the ground for him asking about Julian. I completely missed him going after Mike. That's my fault, but I will do what I can to put it right now."

"Ya think any o' this is your fault?" Julian raised an eyebrow at him. "Don't be so arrogant, Sleuth."

Charlie fidgeted with his buttons and stared at his shoes. The silence grew in weight and discomfort, until

Julian began to narrow his eyes suspiciously at them.

"Look," Charlie muttered, just to break the tension in the air, "I can find the painting. That's not a problem. The problem is, will the Duke let you go and stop threatening Michael if we meet his demands? Or will he just get worse?"

"I 'ave no idea," Julian replied brokenly. "I thought the easiest thing would just be t' kill 'im. Didn't quite pay off."

"I'm surprised he didn't have you arrested for trying," Amy commented.

"Arrested?" Julian grinned at her like there was a sick joke she wasn't privy to. "Man gave me an extra meal and left my bedroom door unlocked. I don' think he's ever been so proud o' me."

"For trying to kill him…?" Amy checked slowly.

"Madness runs in the family, Florin," Charlie commented discretely. "Look at the Duke's grandfather — old Georgie — he was a proper lunatic too."

"At least I know it's hereditary," Julian grimaced. "Don' 'ave t' wonder."

"You're a different flavour of lunacy, Swift," Charlie smiled affectionately.

Julian snorted and gave him a rueful glance. The set of his mouth and pain in his eyes was embarrassed.

"I know ya… ya always looked down on me for it…" he muttered.

"For what?" Charlie scoffed. "Your blue blood? Don't be ridiculous, Swift. That's a fabrication, it's not real. Besides, the making of a person is in their actions. When the revolution comes for the aristocracy, they are not going to hunt down the wayward son who abandoned his wealth, title, and name to flee to London to work in a High House, start a pottery studio, and marry a baker." He stepped closer to the bed, placing a hand to Julian's undamaged cheek and kissing the top of his head. "I've never looked down on you once, Swift. We might have been cut from different cloth, but we're easily the same sail now."

"Careful, Charlie," Julian warned him softly. "Da catches ya kissing me in this house, he will break every bone in ya body and bury ya in the garden to choke to death on blood and dirt."

Amy flinched from the graphic description, but Charlie just nodded like he expected violence of that nature here. Julian slumped further with another broken sigh, his shoulders sagging as he ran his fingers through his hair.

"I messed this up, Sleuth..." he muttered heartbrokenly. "I screwed up so bad, and I got Mike hurt. He's in danger because of me and I don't know how t' get him out. What do I do?"

"Let me see if I can find Denarius," Charlie offered. "We start there and see about getting the painting back. Perhaps, with Florin and I here, we can skew this away from family business and back to some kind of professional deal — buy Mike's freedom."

"Or, bear with me," Julian suggested, "ya could help me just kill the prick and spare the world his existence?"

The offer hung thick and heavy in the air. Everyone could hear the tightness in Charlie's voice when he replied.

"I'm not going to kill anyone, Swift. And I'm not going to ask Florin to be complicit in a murder."

No one challenged him.

"Let me see about Denarius," he repeated. "Florin will stay and look out for you."

"She what?" Julian demanded.

Amy shot her own questioning look at Charlie. Her immediate inclination had not been a polite response, but she kept it back. After all, did she really want to spend the day with Charlie, alone, hunting down an illegal art dealer? Also, perhaps he was trying to make an effort by trusting her with the wellbeing of his friend — who clearly couldn't take care of himself. Charlie didn't look at her. He seemed to try, but his eyes got lost on the way and found his shoes instead. That answered that question.

"I want to have a look at these injuries, Julian," she sighed. "Someone has to watch out for you too, and these look like there might be some fractures — maybe even a concussion."

Julian was staring at them both with barely concealed alarm.

"Why are ya actin' weird?" he demanded. "Is this about the book?"

"What book?" Amy replied, forgetting momentarily after everything else that had happened.

Julian gave her a look and she grimaced.

"Nothing is about the book," she huffed. "The book is not important."

"I disagree," Julian smiled at her. "Ya paint quite the picture, Doc. Love ya depiction of our boy here."

"What depiction of him?" Amy retorted. "No one has any idea what you mean, Julian."

Julian looked between them both, his eyes calculating. Charlie shrugged at him, clearly no wiser in the matter than Amy. The smirk began slowly, but it blossomed into absolute cunning magnificence. Julian grinned at them like a Machiavellian deity who had just gotten into the biscuit tin.

"Ah," was all he said.

Amy decided to ignore him. Charlie followed suit. Julian wasn't letting them get away that easily.

"Did you two 'ave a fight?" he asked.

"No, we did not have a fight," Charlie grumbled. "Give me…" he paused a moment, "two hours. Give me two hours and I'll be right back with the location of the Platine."

"Ya going t' find that painting in two hours?" Julian scoffed.

"I'm going to find out where it is," Charlie replied, already walking back to the door. "Retrieving it will be a completely separate matter, which may require your involvement."

They didn't haggle the details any further and Charlie was already striding from the room. He barely paused in the doorway, and when he did it only seemed to trigger a fresh panic in him before he fled. That left Amy and Julian staring at the empty doorway like imbeciles. She sighed deeply and turned back to her new patient, setting her bag on the side of his bed and opening it up.

"Okay, what's goin' on?" Julian demanded. "What

was that?"

"I wish I knew," Amy sighed, beginning to inspect Julian's injuries. He'd been given a good beating. It almost looked like he'd been in a tavern brawl.

"He won't even look at ya, Amy," Julian pointed out. "Ya didn't turn 'im down, did ya?"

"Me?! Turn him down?!" she scoffed, with a pointed look.

Julian grinned at her. "All right, fair enough. What happened then? Why are ya fightin'?"

"We're not fighting!" she huffed, gently pressing her fingers to his ribs to check for damage. "Breathe in for me, Mister Silver, or whatever you want to call yourself."

"Salty, ain't ya?" Julian commented, wincing as she worked. "I can't believe you won't even tell me. Ya sure it's not about the book?"

Amy thought about that for a moment. Telling Julian wasn't the worst idea. Given what had happened, and how well Julian knew him… and Julian knew the House too.

"What…" she began slowly. "What… do you know… about, um… about Charlie's time living at the High House?"

Julian gave her a very curious look. Amy blushed. She could feel the heat rise through her entire body like someone had lit a fire under her skirt. It was agonising, worse because she knew the embarrassment showed on her face.

"Oh mah God…" Julian grinned at her. "Really?"

"No, shut up," Amy replied instantly, covering his

face with her hand so that he couldn't look at her, and so that she didn't have to see him. He began to laugh behind her hand. "No. It didn't. Get that look off your face, Julian, or I will needle your injuries until you stop."

She could feel the dubious expression beneath her fingers, and wasn't sure if it was because he believed she was a doctor who knew better, or if he thought that's what she was already doing.

Amy heaved a sigh and removed her hands from Julian, dropping them in her lap as she flopped herself down on the bed beside him. They sat shoulder-to-shoulder, staring out the window. She could feel the instant he began to gently side-eye her without moving his head.

"Rebecca booked our tickets and accommodation to follow you," she muttered, staring resolutely out the window. "There was only one room, and only one bed… Julian, stop laughing, or I'm going to smack you."

He was doing his best, but his whole body trembled and his chest fluctuated trying to keep the laughter back.

"You bastard," she muttered under her breath.

"Finally. And what?" Julian chuckled. "Ya want t' know about the House because ya surprised he knew what he was doin'?"

"No," Amy shook her head. "It's not what you think."

"Did ya kiss 'im again?" Julian smirked.

Brushing aside the fact that Julian knew there was an 'again' aspect to it, and ignoring his knowledge of the moment of lunacy at her graduation party, Amy couldn't help but think clinically about it now. Maybe it was because she'd been playing doctor to Julian, who was clearly worse than he was pretending. Charlie had kissed her last night. He had started it this time. There were lots of reasons why he might have reacted the way that he had, but a rather obvious one sprang to mind. It was horrible, and she'd been trying to avoid it, but that just meant she was avoiding him too.

"Julian..." she whispered. "Did... did anyone ever hurt him? Did anything happen to him at the High House when he was a boy?"

"What?" Julian turned to look at her. Amy bit her lip. Julian wasn't laughing anymore. "Amy, what happened?"

"You weren't wholly wrong," she admitted delicately. "Things... got a little heated. He even started it."

"I wanna say 'finally!' but I feel like there's a huge 'but' comin'," Julian said.

"He had a panic attack," Amy sighed. "A big one. The minute I touched him below the belt, he completely freaked out, curled up on the floor, couldn't breathe, didn't want to be touched. I know that there are a lot of reasons he might have reacted that way, I just... God, Julian, I have to ask. Do you know anything? Do you think there's any chance that something happened to him there? He moved in to the House when he was what? Nine? Ten? They were there for four or five years, weren't they—?"

"It didn't happen at the House," Julian insisted.

"I know that was your home too, and I don't want to—"

"It didn't happen at the House," Julian repeated slowly.

Amy paused. She turned to look at him, but Julian was looking at his own fingers, pressing the tips of them together tightly above his knees and flexing the joints.

"Julian…?" Amy whispered with dread.

"Look," he began carefully, "I don't know anythin'. Not properly. I don't know it for sure. No one does. Just a rumour. Mike told me once. Told me I was never allowed t' talk about it. Charlie never told anyone. Never told Mike. Never told his sisters. Never breathed a word. It might just be a rumour."

"Tell me," Amy insisted.

"Rebecca and Susan's wedding," Julian replied. "Rumour has it, Charlie got very drunk that night, woke up in a bed that wasn't his own. Didn't mean to, didn't want to, entirely nonconsensual, but too drunk to know better."

"Charlie?!" Amy was dumbfounded. She thought a moment. "He was only fourteen when Rebecca got married…"

"Aye, yeah, he was," Julian nodded. "Like I said, no one knows about this. As far as the rumours go, I've heard he was basically too drunk t' remember. Also, I don't know for sure there's any truth t' it. Might be complete bollocks."

"Who?" Amy whispered. "Who was he with? Another wedding guest?"

Julian was very quiet for a moment. Every second

that the question hung in the air, Amy could feel it grow colder. It wasn't long before it was icy.

"Julian…?" she whispered.

"Look, I… I only… I only heard the rumour because I was curious about them, y'know?" he muttered. "I was chattin' t' Skipp about it. Thought the relationship was kinda weird, asked him if he knew anythin'. He was terribly reluctant t' say anythin'… but… well, he told me about that. Said he wasn't sure, said Charlie had never mentioned it, but that it maybe explained some of the weirdness. I mean… you ever known an underling t' be so uppity? He'd never get away with that anywhere else."

Amy stared at Julian with a slow, dawning horror. She raised her hands to her mouth.

"Oh my God…" she whispered.

"Aye," Julian nodded. "Ya now know everythin' I do."

"Julian!" Amy exclaimed. "Are you telling me not just that Charlie might have been assaulted, but that if he was, he is still actively living with his abuser?"

"I'm not tellin' ya anythin', because I don't know anythin'," Julian replied. "I am passin' on gossip and rumours, and I thank ya kindly not t' tell anyone ever that I told you anythin'!"

"I won't," she whispered, feeling a little bit like she was going to puke.

They sat in silence for a few moments longer. Amy couldn't think of anything to say while she grappled with the new information. She wasn't sure if Julian regretted telling her. Eventually, she heaved a deep sigh, wondering what she could do to help Julian out of his own predicament. His injuries needed rest more than anything else.

"Amy, can I ask ya a favour?" Julian blurted quietly.

"Of course," she agreed, her mind elsewhere.

"Can I…" Julian could barely get the words out. "Can I get ya medical help wit'… wit' Jamie…?"

"Who's Jamie?" Amy turned to him in surprise.

Julian was leaning with his elbows on his knees, staring at his feet.

"My li'l brother…"

"I didn't know you had a brother," she replied. "Is he hurt? Does he need a doctor?"

"It's complicated…" Julian muttered.

Amy knew that tone. She knew that dread. With a deep and quiet breath, she pulled her clinical veil across her emotions.

"Is he here?" she asked.

"Aye," Julian nodded.

"Then let's go see him," she suggested. As she moved to stand, Julian's hand snatched out and grabbed her wrist. He still wouldn't look up.

"Doc, ya need t' know what I'm askin'," he muttered.

Amy paused and waited for him to elaborate. Julian wet his lips nervously.

"We're gonna 'ave t' break int' a locked room," Julian began slowly, "and just hope he's still alive. Every time I come back up here, I just hope he's still alive. If we get caught doin' what I'm askin', mah Da might very well try an' kill us. If Charlie were here, I wouldn't be askin' because he wouldn't let ya do it."

"Charlie isn't here," Amy replied. "And apparently there are lots of dark things Charlie thinks he alone is allowed to risk. If there is someone in this house who needs my care, I'm a doctor, and by my oath, they get it."

Julian nodded slowly. His hand tentatively began to drop from her arm and he turned his eyes up to face her. The anger was finally gone. The anger and pain about Mike, about his situation, his defensiveness about Charlie… all of it was gone, and he looked so broken and sad she thought her heart would crack.

"Thank ya, Amy," he whispered.

She nodded and waited patiently while he picked himself up from the bed and finished dressing properly. Once he was ready for the day, she let him lead her from the room and up to one of the castle towers.

The stone walls and winding staircase felt painfully familiar. She remembered, with a memory that felt like yesterday and another lifetime all at once, racing up a staircase like this one, in a castle across the channel. This situation bore resemblances she didn't want to think about.

Sure enough, when they reached the door, it was locked and bolted. Julian pulled the bolt and picked the lock as quickly as he could, while Amy kept an ear out for the sound of anyone else coming their way. At least up a long, spiralling tower staircase it was easy enough to hear if someone was coming, and they weren't likely to get incidental traffic.

"Oi! Jamie!" Julian hissed as he popped the door

open.

"Julian?" a hopeful, young voice piped up.

Julian pushed the door ajar and ducked inside, beckoning Amy to follow. The bedroom behind wasn't too dissimilar to Julian's, and a scruffily dressed boy on the other side collided with Julian's chest like he'd been shot out of a cannon. Amy winced just to see it happen, thinking of Julian's bruises, but Julian took it in his stride, wrapping the kid in his arms.

"I thought ya might be dead!" Jamie exclaimed.

"Not yet," Julian hugged his little brother tightly. He didn't say more, but his eyes spoke volumes of concern that death was the fear he carried in abundance for the boy he was embracing. She could almost see in the set of his jaw and the tension of his eyes, Julian never said 'goodbye'. His farewell was more likely to be 'stay alive'.

"Da said ya tried t' kill him…" Jamie added.

"Aye," Julian admitted, squeezing Jamie once. "Sorry I didn't manage it."

"We'll get 'im next time," Jamie promised.

"We'll get 'im next time," Julian agreed.

"I was just worried he got ya instead," Jamie muttered.

"That old bastard? Na," Julian smiled grimly. "Think he's actually proud'a me, messed up soggy shite that he is. Been waitin' for me t' try for years."

Julian let his brother go with a sigh and Amy regarded them. She could see instantly the resemblance between the brothers… and the problem. Jamie looked up at her with big dark eyes, half-terrified and half-curious. She'd never had a child look at her in terror before.

"Hi Jamie," she smiled gently, trying to appear as safe as possible. "I'm Doctor Amelia Florin, and I'm a friend of Julian's. He's asked me if I could check up on any injuries you might have and see if I can fix anything for you."

Jamie immediately looked to Julian for security. Julian nodded reassuringly.

"Aye, she's good, Jamie," he promised.

Jamie wore an oversized shirt tucked into baggy trousers. His clothes were ill-fitting and looked like they were probably Julian's hand-me-downs. He hugged his torso anxiously as he looked between the adults.

"How old are you, Jamie?" Amy asked.

"Twelve," he muttered in a tiny voice.

"Twelve can be a tricky age," Amy offered sympathetically. "I'm guessing you're running into some new problems."

"Just mah Da," Jamie shrugged bitterly.

"Okay," Amy nodded. "You all right with me taking a look?"

Jamie didn't put up any kind of fight. He went over and perched on the edge of his bed, undressing the top half of his body. Amy wanted to cry when she saw, but she steeled herself professionally and took it in stride. Jamie had long curls down to his shoulders, they hid his face as he waited for examination, and Amy couldn't help but wonder if he was the reason Julian grew his own hair — to encourage his brother.

"Okay, Jamie," Amy said slowly, carefully looking

him over without touching him. "Can you tell me how much of this bruising is from your dad and how much is from your binding?"

Jamie shrugged. "No idea."

Amy grimaced. The kid's torso was black and blue and it was hard to tell were one bruise finished and the next started. Some of them were clearly from beatings, but some looked like they might have been self-inflicted — incidentally or otherwise. She took a deep breath and clasped her hands to keep them from trembling.

"Okay, sweetheart, I can get you some better cloth and teach you some different binding techniques that will be kinder to your body, but — you want my professional opinion?" she looked between the brothers. "We need to get you out of this house. Your biggest threat to your health right now is your father."

"Shite, really? I hadn't thought o' that," Julian drawled sarcastically.

Amy glared at him.

"I can't," Jamie shook his head. "If I try and leave, he'll kill me — an' mah Ma."

"Not if we kill 'im first..." Julian muttered.

"Someone's coming!" Jamie whispered, quickly throwing his shirt back on.

Everyone froze and listened. Julian looked like he was getting ready to kick whoever came through the doorway back down the stairs, but Jamie motioned to him and shook his head. Light but firm footsteps approached the room and the door was pushed wide. Amy recognised the butler from earlier. He gave them all a severe look and a sigh.

"I might've known," he concluded. "I've been looking for you, Rory. You and your friends are expected for lunch. You know what happens if you disappoint?"

Julian closed his eyes in reluctant acknowledgement, and Jamie flinched tellingly. The butler eyed the younger brother.

"Mary," he addressed Jamie, "if you could do your best not to cause a scene today. I imagine things will be tense enough."

He didn't stick around for replies. Certainly not long enough for the lecture Amy wanted to deliver. Half of her couldn't believe a servant could be so rude, especially after Julian's comments downstairs; but half of her realised that everyone in his house lived on the edge of a blade. They behaved this way because they were just trying to survive. She was so busy worrying about the Sovereign brothers and how to help them, she wasn't even dwelling on the fact that she was about to have to endure an entire luncheon with their father. At least Charlie had implied he'd be back by then.

9

Charlie was indeed back in time for lunch, although abruptly aware that there were many other, and far more pleasant, activities he could have chosen to spend his time involved in — like being the victim of defenestration or hot-coal walking. He was wound tighter than an anxious man's watch and desperately calculating how to manage the situation with minimal disaster.

He had barely had time to inform Amy and Julian that he had successfully tracked down Denarius and recruited her aid, before they were called into a lunch that nobody wanted to attend. Amy looked worse than when he left her, and Charlie felt like he was going to drown in guilt. If Hell was a real place, this was it, and the guilt was going to torture him for eternity. Not just for what he'd already done to her, but what he was worried he was about to do.

He couldn't stop thinking about last night… about the feel of her, and the taste of her, and how badly he'd wanted her, until—

And then his chest began to tighten and his lungs shrank again. His breathing became shallow and all he could do was focus on it and try not to black out.

And try not to remember something else.

Something dark.

A hot, dark room and the overwhelming scent of champagne.

The memory made him start to gag. He pushed it away. Far away. It wasn't a problem if he didn't let it be. Besides, he had the aristocracy to fight.

Albert Sovereign was the spitting image of Julian — except thirty years older, twice the size, and with a full beard. He had the bloodshot eyes of a drunk, overcome with a truly sadistic madness. Charlie had seen the like before, but he had not had the pleasure of the Duke in person until today.

Charlie calculated the other attendees at the table. Duke Sovereign was appropriately seated at the head of the table. Charlie and Amy were down one side, and Charlie did not like that Amy was the one seated next to the Duke. Across from them, were the Duke's second son Jamie and wife Anne. Charlie had been sizing them up.

Jamie was outfitted ridiculously in a dress that did its best to be overtly feminine (a description which would have flummoxed Charlie had he not been witnessing it) and which seemed to be deeply humiliating and uncomfortable for the poor boy, who barely knew how to hold himself. His mother, whom Charlie knew was Julian's step-mother, was the ghost of a once beautiful woman. She sat demurely, never made eye contact with anyone, never spoke unless spoken to — and even then only timid and brief responses, and she flinched any time Sovereign moved his hands.

Julian sat down the other end of the table, between Charlie and Jamie, and the hate and anger that radiated off him was palpable. If Charlie had been in the mood to try toxicity, he could have spread it on his bread. If he was honest, he could feel a similar energy wafting off Amy. Her face was pinched in fury and part of him regretted leaving her behind. All of him regretted bringing her to Scotland.

Now they were stuck here, having lunch with an abused family, both of them trying not to start something that would only endanger the victims further, while they listened to the deep and resonant bigotry of a tyrant demeaning and deadnaming both his children.

"So, *the* Shilling an' Florin," Duke Sovereign eyeballed them. "I remember ya, lass. Mister Shilling... ya a lot smaller than I thought ya'd be."

"I get that a lot," Charlie nodded politely.

Sovereign grunted. "Rory hired ya to fix his mistake then?"

"Actually, we're here on our own business," Charlie replied carefully, trying to maintain the illusion of emotional distance from Julian in the hope that it would protect him — or at least deny his father another weapon to use against him. "We're working for the man you had attacked."

"What?" Sovereign squinted at him. "That faggot baker?"

Charlie felt Amy's hand fly across his waist beneath the table, attempting to pin him in his chair. He didn't move, but her hand was hot across his stomach and he tried to ignore the wave of dizziness it brought on. Julian was the one who looked like he was about to commit a murder.

"Come on, Da," he taunted. "Ya got better insults than that."

"Why waste 'em?" Sovereign smirked at him.

"Because that baker is where ya Platine money is goin'," Julian retorted. "An' once I'm done 'ere, I might take a few more fancy things t' spend on 'im."

"Try me, lad," Sovereign warned. "I will 'ave someone chop him int' little bits an' feed 'im t' ya."

"There's no need for threats, Da," Julian smirked. "I eat 'im for fun, no mutilation required."

"No' at the table, Rory!" Sovereign snorted in disgust.

"Oh, I'm sorry, does the thought of me sucking cock upset ya?" Julian grinned.

"Rory..." Sovereign warned in a deadly tone.

"What?!" Julian bellowed at him, leaning on the table. "What, Da? Ya already swore t' kill 'im. Ya only doin' it because he scares ya."

"Scared?!" Sovereign roared. "Of that —"

"You are terrified!" Julian yelled back. "It scares the absolute shite outta ya t' think of me with a man. That's why you've been such a prick about it mah whole life! Well, ya fears are valid, Da, because I do. I take it, an' I like it!"

"Rory!"

"I love it! An' I love 'im! An' I'm gonna take a Goddamn pound o' flesh for every scar ya gave 'im!"

Julian bellowed.

Duke Sovereign grabbed a knife and hurled it down the table at Julian. Charlie reacted on instinct. The entire fight felt like it had been escalating in slow motion, right down to Duchess Anne cowering behind her hands as things took a turn. Charlie lashed out and caught the knife as it went by. Everyone froze.

"Sorry, instincts," he apologised, setting the knife carefully down on the table in front of him.

The moment hovered, caught between exploding and settling, and he had no idea how to shift it to further de-escalation. All hopes of being able to reason with a man like Sovereign were disintegrating to ash. Then Amy cleared her throat.

"Goodness," she commented, "family lunches haven't been this intense since Harry died."

The words hovered for a moment, and then Sovereign began to laugh. A strange and different unease settled at the table and Charlie felt his chest tighten again. He didn't like the look on Amy's face. There was a smile, but it was dark. Everything about it was dark and twisted, as though something awful was happening inside her to allow her to meet Sovereign's eye without fear. The Duke met her look with a warm twinkle and a chuckle. Charlie wanted to puke.

"Aye," Sovereign nodded. "I heard about that. Very funny. The Lord Chief Justice raised a serial killer. Who'da thought?"

"No one, for a very long time," Amy replied, an ironic twist to her mouth like she got the joke.

Charlie didn't. He didn't understand what was

happening at all. Sovereign eyeballed them both with a smirk.

"So's it true, then?" he pried. "You were shagging the detective who caught him? Just happened t' catch ya fiancé red-handed?"

"Not at all," Amy replied cooly. "I'm afraid rumours of our affair have been greatly exaggerated — one could say outright fabricated. I was using Mister Shilling for a different kind of personal matter."

"An' not shy about it," Sovereign chuckled. "Y'know, last time we met, lass, I don't recall Pound's bastard being so confident."

Amy immediately put her hand back on Charlie's waist. He hadn't even realised he'd started to stand. There had just been a flash of red for a moment and then she was touching him and reality came back into focus.

"Not Pound's bastard, Your Grace," she replied. "Doctor Florin."

"I dunno who ya think ya kidding, lass," Sovereign laughed. "Ya mother might'a been married t' Henry's brother, but no one believes ya his child."

"No, but that's what I was using Charlie for," Amy retorted.

Everyone at the table was taken aback in surprise. Amy appeared to consider that, and then began to elaborate at her own pace.

"You may have heard, Your Grace, of our elopement to Paris?" Amy postured. "Well, knowing there was not so much as a shred of truth to the elopement might pose the question: what were we actually doing? The truth of the matter was I had Mister Shilling here help me find my birth parents. My mother was certainly a con-woman, that part is true, but my father is a French Marquis, and they were legally married. Hence, I may have been adopted by Lord Pound, but I am nobody's bastard."

"Fascinatin'," Sovereign mused. "And ya still workin' together? Comin' up 'ere after Rory?"

"Someone had to," Amy replied. "We are interested in buying the freedom of Michael Pence. I understand that the price is the Platine painting you lost?"

"Are ya sayin', lass, that you an' ya wee pocket detective are gonna find mah paintin' for me?" Sovereign eyed her calculatingly.

"That depends," she countered coolly. "I have no interest in helping someone who doesn't help me."

Sovereign's answering smile left a cold and uncomfortable sweat across Charlie's back. He wanted to grab Amy and make a dash for the door before whatever horrible thing he could feel approaching arrived. Julian got there first.

"Don't trust 'im, Amy," Julian ordered. "Whatever he says, don't trust 'im."

"Jesus Christ, Rory!" Sovereign snapped. "Behave, for five minutes, ya li'l shite!"

"I'll behave, Da," Julian glared, "when I finally bury ya cold, dead body so deep that not even the worms'll have ya. Li'l buggers don't deserve t' be poisoned with ya foulness."

Sovereign gave that a contemplative and respectful nod. "Not bad," he complimented. "Ya been savin' that one?"

"Do not act like mah insults buy ya love, Da," Julian spat. "Ya don't have any love. Ya never did. Ya own mother, God rest her, couldn't love somethin' as evil as you."

Sovereign rolled his eyes. "There's the drama, again, Rory. Always the drama with ya. I'm doin' what's best for ya."

"You 'ave never done anythin' good for me mah entire life!" Julian screamed at him, half rising in outrage.

"Sit ya arse down!" Sovereign bellowed. "I made you, Rory. I moulded you, and I will do whatever it takes t' make sure ya ready when I need ya t' be. You are mah only heir—"

"Jamie is right there!" Julian screamed, thrusting an arm towards his younger brother. "Ya insanity needs a male heir? Jamie is sitting right there, Da!"

"*Mary*," Sovereign leant on the name with so much venom it became toxic to touch, "is mah daughter and not fit to inherit. That said, should she bear a son when she's married, that's a different story."

"When she's married…" Julian repeated like he was being forced to swallow dog shit. "So the threat o' disownin' me and leavin' mah step-mother and li'l brother to starve in the cold finally goes out the window if you can find another cock t' fill ya gap? An' I'm the faggot, Da? Really?"

"Go on, Rory," Sovereign taunted. "Take the out. Ya want it so bad? Ya spend all ya time gripin' that ya don't want it — let Mary's kids swipe ya crown."

"There are no kids and there is no crown, you mangy

old c—"

"She's gettin' married!" Sovereign cut him off. "She hadn't told ya? I've been in talks with Lord Airgid, he's comin' by next week t' finalise the deal."

For a moment everyone was completely frozen. Charlie didn't know who to stare at and couldn't help but glance at everyone. The glances told him everything. He wished they didn't. He wished he didn't notice things. He wished he couldn't see the way that Amy's confidant veil had shredded, the blood draining from her face as she lost the will to maintain face in front of the Duke; or little Jamie, who was nearly catatonic trying to suppress a complete emotional and mental breakdown; or Jamie's mother Anne, who looked like she was ready to throw herself on her own pyre.

"Jamie's twelve..." Julian said numbly.

Sovereign looked at him like he was waiting for Julian to make a point.

"Da... Jamie's twelve! He's twelve! Airgid's in 'is fifties! Da! Da, ya can't—!"

"Mary's had her first blood," Sovereign cut him off. "She can be married."

"Your Grace," Amy blurted, looking rather faint, "modern medical recommendations suggest—"

"Do not come t' mah house, lass, and try an' tell me 'ow t' raise mah family," Sovereign warned her.

"Ya can't do this!" Julian roared at him, getting to his feet.

"Sit down!" Sovereign bellowed.

Julian didn't sit and the two of them continued screaming at each other until the room was just a storm of noise. There were no discernible words, just the cacophony of sound. Both of them yelling themselves blue in the face. Charlie could see Amy trying to catch Jamie's eye, trying to reassure the child. Then Sovereign stood to face Julian. The whole table flinched when he got to his feet.

"This is ya problem, lad!" he roared. "Ya weak, pussy shite! Ya all talk. Ya always 'ave been! Nothin' else in ya! Ya been sayin' ya'll kill me for so long it's lost all meanin'. There's no threat there."

"I swear, in the eyes o' God, Da," Julian panted. "Ya try marryin' Jamie t' that ol' bastard, I will gut ya both like fish."

Sovereign shook his head in disappointment.

"Ya been sayin' shite like that ya whole life, Rory," he scolded. "Ya threatened me anytime I disciplined you or the others, and ya not done shite. Ya said ya'd kill me when I banned ya from them boys at the brothel—"

"Ya took me down there!" Julian yelled. "It's not mah fault ya didn't like what happened!"

"—ya said ya'd burn me alive when I broke the legs o' that stable boy I caught ya with," Sovereign reminded. "Same as ya doin' now. Ya told me ya'd stab me in the back when ya mother fell down those stairs... terrible tragedy."

Julian snatched a knife from the table and everyone drew back. Everyone except the Duke. Julian was glaring at him down the length of the table like a provoked dog, teeth bared in a snarl of pure hatred. Duke Sovereign was smiling. It was a cruel and taunting expression. Sadistic in every way.

"An' this is the problem, Rory," he scoffed. "How'd I raise such a coward? Ya want t' take that knife and stab me in the 'eart right now, and not a single person at this table would dream of stoppin' ya, but ya won't because ya chicken shite. Li'l pussy Rory. All talk an' no action. Not for ya baker, not for ya sister, not for ya mother. Ya spineless."

"Why do ya want me t' kill ya so bad?!" Julian demanded.

"I wanna know ya not a pussy, Rory!" Sovereign roared at him. "I wanna know ya got it in ya! I wanna know ya can look at this fight, know ya gonna lose it, an' do it anyway! Where's the boy who gave me this?" Sovereign motioned to a bruise, the very edges just visible beneath his thick, salted, dark beard. "I know he's in there, Rory. Where is he?!"

The two men stared each other down. Finally, Julian tightened his grip on the knife. Sovereign grinned at him. Charlie tensed, waiting to leap forward. Julian drove the knife as hard as he could into the table, stabbing it deep into the polished wood, never breaking eye-contact.

"Not on your terms," he swore, a trace of his London accent healing over his ragged voice. He stood tall, pushing his chair back as he stepped away from the table. "Never on your terms."

"Rory!" Sovereign roared at him as he walked away. "Rory! Ya chicken shite li'l—!"

Julian slammed the door with shuddering force on the whole room. Charlie wished he'd gone with him, but there were more important things to consider. Without Julian there to provoke the Duke, the dust began to settle in the room. It helped that no one else appeared to be breathing. Sovereign took his seat again and reached for his goblet, taking a loud, slurping gulp of wine.

"Sovereign," Charlie addressed the Duke carefully, instantly feeling the atmosphere ice over with dread. "I have business I wish to discuss with you, and I fear that all the excitement may have upset the delicate disposition of our ladies. I don't supposed the two of us could continue our conversation without company?"

The Duke seemed to consider this. With barely a glance, he gave the order.

"Get out." It wasn't even a snap, just a dismissal.

Charlie shared a glance with Amy. It was nice to meet her eye again, in circumstances that were dire enough to wash away their own concerns. Her eyes were fearful and warning, but he met them calmly. They both knew they needed to take advantage of Sovereign's bigotry to get his wife and child out of the room. Amy gave him a half-nod to show she understood as she slowly got to her feet. Then she and Anne took charge of silently ushering Jamie from the room. Only once the door was shut, and Charlie had trapped himself alone in the room with Albert Sovereign, did he allow himself to begin considering his options.

"Go on, Shilling," the Duke taunted. "Ya got what ya wanted. What's next?"

Charlie pursed his lips in thought. Sovereign was

nasty — a special breed of absolute maliciousness — but he wasn't stupid. He knew Charlie was trying to protect other people. He knew Charlie was full of weak spots. And he knew Charlie was so full of loathing, not just for him but for the very concept of the aristocracy, that Charlie had not yet been able to address him as 'Your Grace' even when introduced to him. Right now, there was no point beating around the bush.

"Michael Pence's life for the Platine," Charlie replied. "That's all I'm here for. It's all I've been hired for."

"It's all ya *want*," Sovereign taunted. "Don't forget that part, Mister Shilling. Ya 'ave all ya cards on the table, an' ya not holdin' that many."

"The one I'm holding is the one you desire," he replied. "That makes it plenty."

"No," Sovereign shook his head, taking another long slurp from his cup. "Because ya want ya friend t' be safe a lot more than I want mah stolen property back, don't ya? I know I can get more outta ya than one paintin'."

Charlie was silent while he considered this. He had hoped to be able to play this as a job, present it as a simple transaction, but Sovereign already knew better.

"What do you want?" he replied, getting straight to the point.

"Return mah Platine," Sovereign ordered. "Show me ya as good as ya reputation. Then, ya want that baker's life? We'll talk more."

10

When Charlie finally escaped the Duke, he found Amy and Julian hiding away in Julian's bedroom — a notion that would have delighted his father, if it hadn't also been so completely innocuous. The instant he entered the room, Amy flew at him and embraced him around the chest. He waited for the panic to hit him, but it never did. He slowly put his arms around her too, and held her close. Apparently, the incident last night was behind them, for now. The feeling of her was comforting and the scent of her perfume soothing. He hadn't realised how terrified he had felt in the absence of her friendship until it was holding him steady again.

"Thank God," Julian muttered. "I was worried I was gonna 'ave t' come get ya."

"I don't think he means me any particular ill will yet," Charlie sighed, still holding Amy and wondering when would be the appropriate moment to let her go. "What happened to your family?"

"Ya mean Jamie an' Anne?" Julian replied. "Upstairs. Anne's lookin' after Jamie. Thought we'd give them some space. Obviously, they're not doin' so good."

"Did you at least manage to strike a deal for

Michael?" Amy asked, slipping back from the embrace but still holding Charlie by the shoulders.

He met her eye and wished he hadn't. She saw right through him, saw all his struggle and disappointment.

"He won't discuss a deal for Skipp until the painting is returned," Charlie muttered.

"Can't ya just—" Julian mimed garrotting someone.

"Julian!" Amy exclaimed, placing a protective hand over Charlie, like she was trying to shield him.

Charlie sighed to himself. There was no shielding from that. There didn't deserve to be.

"We can't just go about killing every horrible person we disagree with," he muttered.

"Not even if someone contacts Pound so ya can get his blessing for this one?" Julian retorted.

"Excuse me?!" Amy demanded. "Firstly, Julian, watch what you're implying, and secondly, if you want someone dead that badly, why aren't you doing it yourself? If your father can sit up here and commit crime after crime with no one stopping him — if he can threaten Michael, and abuse Jamie and Anne, and assault people, cripple and kill people! — then surely the next Duke could get away with disposing of him. Not that I am trying to encourage you, far from it, but I will not stand by while you demand someone else commit crimes on your behalf. Shame on you, Julian."

Julian keeled slightly sideways to better meet Charlie's eye.

"I think she likes ya," he smirked.

"I know you're deflecting because you can't cope with what's happening, Swift," Charlie sighed. "But we have to work out how we're going to protect Skipp from your dad."

"I thought mah plan was excellent," Julian huffed, flopping back on his bed without a care for his injuries.

Charlie and Amy ignored him. Her hand was still on his chest and she showed no inclination to move it. It was warm and comforting and part of him wanted to draw into it. He wanted to pull her back into his arms and hold her until everything was all right again. Until they were all right again.

Unfortunately, things were more likely to go wrong for them before they went right.

"Florin, I'm going to need you to come with me to retrieve the painting," he murmured.

She looked at him in concern. He could think of at least six reasons why she could be looking at him like that and had no idea which one was responsible.

"Ya can just say ya wanna get her out o' the house, Sleuth," Julian called from the bed. "No one'd blame ya."

Charlie looked away from them all, scratching the side of his nose nervously and moving back from Amy's touch. He could feel a frown pulling at the edges of his mouth.

"It wasn't you I was watching, Swift," Charlie sighed.

"What now?" Julian sat up on the edge of the bed.

"I knew about the Platine, but it wasn't because I was keeping an eye on you," he admitted reluctantly. "I had been keeping tabs on Denarius, so your transaction got flagged. That's how I knew about it."

"Denarius?" Julian echoed. "Huh. She seemed perfectly respectable."

"She always does," Charlie commented.

"That's why you didn't let me go with you earlier!" Amy exclaimed, pointing an accusatory finger at Charlie. He took it in stride, nodding acceptingly. He did deserve it. "Elizabeth Denarius! I should have known."

"To your credit," Charlie attempted to placate her, "I believe roughly 22 percent of women in Britan are called Elizabeth, and Denarius is even more common. It's not exactly a suspicious name."

"She's agreed to help? What are you giving her in return?" Amy demanded.

"I'm afraid I agreed to the pleasure of your company," Charlie admitted. "I did, however, specify very plainly that I would not promise an agreeable encounter. You do not have to play nice for her, but all she asked was that she be allowed to see you. There's a tea house in the city, she made a reservation for 3pm. I… may have agreed to take you to meet her." Charlie paused and regarded his companions. "That was before I was aware of the lunch, of course."

"What's goin' on?" Julian inquired.

"You may recall at lunch I mentioned Charlie had helped me uncover my birth parents?" Amy reminded with a pertinent look. "Well, Julian, the con-woman you fenced that painting through was my mother."

The refurbished tea rooms at the Jenner's department store were modern and popular. Amy did not blame her mother for picking such a public place to meet. At least it would encourage Amy not to slap her across the face when she saw her again. Half of her knew it wasn't worth it. It wasn't worth her time, energy, or grief. But half of her would always hold a special sliver of white-hot pain for the woman who had abandoned her at birth.

At least she had Charlie with her, and at least he was behaving normally. Well, normal for Charlie. He walked her up the stairs with her hand cupped around his elbow. If Tanner's camera had been anywhere in the vicinity, it would have had a field day.

"You don't have to stay," he murmured as they scoured the seating arrangements between the pillars for any sign of 'Elizabeth Denarius'. "You can say 'hello' and 'goodbye' and just leave."

"Oh, I think I have a bit more to say to her than just that," Amy replied, unable to keep the attitude from her tone. She was all too aware of the sidelong glance Charlie cast her way, and the discrete but admiring smile that teased his lips. He was doing his best to be supportive. She wanted to kiss him again. She wanted to throw her arms around his neck and press her lips to his adorably crooked mouth in a way that would scandalise bystanders.

But there was a part of her that couldn't shift the imagery Julian had conjured for her with his rumours. There was a part of her that ached for him in an entirely different way. She would credit him thus — before she had befriended Charlie Shilling, she'd had no idea the human heart could bleed in so many different ways.

It caught a new wound as they came around a partition and found Denarius sitting alone at one of the rectangular four-person tables. She had her back to them and didn't see them approach, for which Amy was grateful. She had thought herself prepared for this reunion, and did not anticipate the immediate stabbing sensation in her chest when she saw her mother sitting at the table.

She could feel the tears she had wept at her mother's letter on the way home from France burning the back of her throat, and she swallowed them down like fire. Charlie's fingers tightened over her own reassuringly. Perhaps he had felt her hand tighten on his arm. Perhaps he had noticed some other traitorous sign — that way that he always did.

Something about their approach must have betrayed them, because Denarius turned and stood as they neared.

"Amelia, darling," she gushed, beaming and holding out her arms like they were a regular mother and daughter who did tea every week.

Amy had a swathe of different visions for how this might have gone, but all her fantasies melted away in the face of the real thing, and she found she had neither the wit nor the temperament to initiate any of them.

"That's a very warm welcome from someone who never bothered to say goodbye," she retorted softly, too cautious to cause a scene and too icy to pretend things were fine.

Elizabeth read the room and dropped the façade. Her eyes washed over them, calculatingly taking in Amy's frosty expression. A wave of undisguised amusement crossed over her face as she eyed up Charlie, like she found the defensiveness of his stance entertaining. The smile stayed as she looked back at Amy, meeting her gaze.

"Maybe I'm trying to make up for that," she replied.

"Which time?" Amy countered. "When you abandoned me as a baby or when I got to meet you for the first time in my life and you vanished in the middle of the night?"

Elizabeth took that on the chin politely and held her tongue. She held a hand out invitingly toward the table, encouraging them to sit. Amy paused a moment, but the choice was hers alone and neither of the others pushed her into it. Charlie didn't move until she did, and then he followed her lead to the table. She was certain that if she had turned around he would have followed her lead out the door too, which was remarkably compassionate given that his friends' lives hung in the balance of this transaction. But given that, knowing that Michael and Julian were in danger, Amy couldn't just walk out — even if she'd wanted to. In truth, she didn't. She moved to the table and let Charlie pull out her chair for her.

"Aren't you two just the cutest," Elizabeth commented, joining them at the table.

"No," Amy snapped, instantly sensing Charlie's discomfort at the remark. "We're colleagues."

Elizabeth laughed and then seemed to realise it wasn't supposed to be a joke. Amy stared her down, lounging judgementally in her chair with her legs crossed beneath her skirts. Her foot rested gently against the side of Charlie's calf beneath the table, and he made no move to shy away from her. His eyes were also on Elizabeth, and just as stern. Although, his gaze was warning, not angry. Amy's mother tried to backpaddle her amusement, and didn't completely fail, even if she couldn't quite quash her smirk.

A waiter came by with a fresh pot of tea, attractive chinaware, and a plate of small cakes. Denarius had clearly ordered before they'd arrived, but she'd ordered like she'd had no doubt they would be joining her. She flirted softly with the waiter, but neither Amy nor Charlie said a word and the tension was satisfyingly stiff.

"I must say," Elizabeth began again, pouring them all tea once they were alone, "I'm surprised to find you back in my business, especially given the legitimacy of my current dealings."

"You just sold a stolen painting," Amy reminded tartly.

"It was a possession of Duke Sovereign and his heir had me sell it," Elizabeth shrugged. "What the Duke and his son have going on between them is their business."

"Now it's ours," Amy replied. "The Duke is threatening to have one of our friends killed if he doesn't get his painting back."

"So Mister Shilling said," Elizabeth smiled at him.

Amy did not like the way her mother smiled at Charlie. It made her want to upend the table and storm out. Fortunately, Charlie was Charlie, and whatever charms Amy's mother appeared to have on most of mankind, Charlie was utterly immune to them. He didn't even seem to notice. Elizabeth was still smirking at them like they were a cute joke only she was in on, but she made an effort to hide the amusement behind her teacup. "If there's blackmail and murder involved, have you told your father about it?" she asked, quickly clarifying, "Lord Pound, I mean, not Jacques — although I'm certain Jacques would be happy to run a man through for you, darling."

"I haven't told either of them," Amy replied. "Sovereign is royalty. There's not much they can do. Everyone knows he's a monster and they've done nothing about it. The Queen hasn't even bothered to disown him. I don't know how to take him down within the law."

Denarius regarded them both for a long interval. Even Amy couldn't outstare her this time, not after she'd just admitted she didn't know how to resolve her predicament. Regardless of the fact that no one else knew how to solve it either. Reluctantly, she sipped at her tea, which was altogether too delicious and relaxing for such a strained affair. Charlie sat beside her like a scruffy but unwavering guard terrier. Denarius pushed the plate of baking towards him.

"Have a cake, Charlie," she invited. Immediately, she shook her head to dispel more laughter at his expression. "They're not poisoned, darling. You're just even scrawnier than I remember."

Amy felt a strong urge to defend him, but decided that admitting to her mother that she'd seen Charlie shirtless was as appealing as attending another meal with the Sovereigns.

"You have the look of a woman who's about to do something we'll regret," Charlie told her. Amy hid her own smile behind her mug.

"No, Mister Shilling," Elizabeth shook her head. "I have the look of someone who is prepared to make your problem go away."

"We just want the painting—" he began.

"No, you want Sovereign to leave you and your friends alone," Elizabeth cut him off. "The painting has nothing to do with that, Duke Sovereign just made you think it does. Someone with power like that doesn't relinquish it because you do an odd job for them."

Amy glanced at Charlie. He'd already said that much. He caught her eye and they shared a look. Denarius was right. Charlie sat back, his defensiveness wearing thin, and picked up his tea.

"Why are you helping us?" Amy demanded.

"Because, like it or not, you're my daughter," Elizabeth replied, her voice tightening ever so slightly in a way that Amy would have considered telling in anyone else. It was telling here too, but she couldn't bring herself to read it, not even when Elizabeth continued. "I know I never did right by you, but I tried, Amelia, I truly did. I knew I couldn't care for you. I knew I couldn't take you back to your father. I left you in the best place I could find, with a good man who would care for you far better than I could have. I never thought my heart could break more than it did that night, not until I had to do it again. And you can hate me for that, but Jacques had kept me locked in that tower for weeks, and he told me my only guarantee of freedom was to leave then and never return. I'm sorry I wasn't strong enough to risk imprisonment for you. I'm sorry I wasn't strong enough to risk my life for you. You can hate me if you want to, but you are my daughter, and I will do whatever I can now to do right by you this time."

It felt like the letter all over again and, hearing her say it, Amy was forced to detach herself completely to avoid dissolving into tears at the table. She wanted to melt. She wanted to become rain and wash the Earth of grief. Of herself. Of this stranger she had become who was woven of loss.

"What..." she whispered, hearing the thick heaviness of her struggling voice like treacle poured from tin, "what does that look like?"

Elizabeth blinked at her, taking a deep slow breath. Amy realised she was also trying not to cry. She wanted to do something to lighten the mood, to pretend that they weren't carrying so much emotional baggage. She and Charlie drank their tea while they let Denarius take a moment to compose her answer calmly.

"Right now, it looks like me helping you out with Sovereign," Elizabeth answered. "You're my little girl, so the only man who gets to take advantage of you is our boy Charlie here."

Shilling and Florin both choked on their drinks.

Elizabeth snorted at them in amusement as they coughed and gagged and composed themselves. Amy snatched at a napkin to dab carefully at her lips and chin. Charlie wiped his mouth with the back of his hand and looked like someone had just slapped him. Elizabeth was still grinning at them. Amy glared. Her mother had had entirely too much fun with that.

"Sovereign isn't after Amy," Charlie grumbled.

"Give it thirty minutes," Denarius retorted. "Besides, whatever con you two think you're pulling has fooled no one. Sovereign messing with you, Shilling, is messing with my Amelia — whether you see it or not. Now, you can't affect him within the law. However, working outside the law is my area of expertise. Sometimes you need a crook to take down another crook." Her voice was firm and certain again, but a softness overcame her eyes as she looked at Amy. "I don't know if you ever got my letter, but I meant it, darling. Every word. I'm happy to do this."

"What does that look like?" Amy repeated.

"It looks like having tea and cake, and then going to visit the Duke," Denarius replied.

11

The tea and cake were very good, but Amy could not shift the sensation that things were… strange. Having a mother like this, a relationship like this, it was something she had always wanted. Not that she had allowed herself to consider it for many years now. Plenty of people were raised by a single parent. She and Harry had… well, she wanted to say managed just fine. Perhaps bringing Harry into it made for a bad example. Nevertheless, regardless of what had happened with Harry, there was a part of Amy that had always yearned for this. Now that she had it, it felt very… odd.

She would be the first to admit this was not a normal relationship. But then, what was? She didn't have any normal relationships. She was sitting, now, in a carriage with her mother and Charlie, heading back up to the Sovereign Estate. Elizabeth was trying to pretend things were fine. Charlie was having none of it, his eyes ever wary of her. Amy sat next to him, wanting things to be fine but unable to live the lie. The discomfort of the situation caused her to draw close to Charlie for reassurance, and he showed no reservations. Only maintained his protective air.

That meant they were sitting too close. Denarius

could see. Amy knew she should move away, but she couldn't make herself do it. What was the point? Her mother already thought they were an item. Given her comment at the tearoom, she probably thought they were sleeping together. A hot wave washed over Amy at the thought of Elizabeth finding out about the room at the inn. She couldn't even imagine how she'd explain that to anyone else.

She was still dwelling on it as they pulled up the drive. That meant she was the last to notice. She should have noticed when they reached the Estate to find the gate open and unguarded, but she was too distracted. Charlie perked up first. His head cocked and he peered intently out the window. That was such normal behaviour for him that it didn't register as an event. Then Elizabeth got curious too.

"Something exciting seems to be happening," she commented.

Amy followed their gazes. There was a police wagon and uniformed officers outside the house, along with a large number of the Estate staff. None of the Sovereign family were present.

"Julian!" Charlie gasped. He banged on the back wall of the carriage. "Stop! Stop here!" he yelled, opening the door before the carriage finished halting. He was out the door and bolting up the rest of the drive before anyone could stop him.

"Charlie!" Amy called, giving chase. She hurried out of the carriage, but found herself inadvertently falling behind. She didn't want to see this. She couldn't make herself run towards it. God, watching him run... he was sprinting like he knew something she didn't. She could deduce from the police presence and the clear shock of the staff that something big had happened. But it was Charlie's speed that told her someone was dead.

If Charlie got to the top of the drive and found his friend dead… Amy did not want to see what would happen next. If she got to the top of the drive and found Anne or Jamie dead… she did not know what she'd do next. All she did know was that she would not hold herself accountable for her own actions.

Charlie was disappearing around the side of the house when Amy reached the crowd. She was surprised they were admitted, until she realised they had already been introduced as Shilling and Florin. The staff had all but been waiting for them, and the police had been forewarned they were coming. The guard from the gate was standing by, wringing his cap in his hands, and he gave her a very direct look.

She followed Charlie around to the cordoned scene. He was stopped just outside the barrier. She stopped at his shoulder. Broken glass was strewn across the cobbled ground and blood was everywhere. The mangled body was crumpled on the ground far beneath the tower window.

Charlie was paused, head tilted, absolutely frozen, considering the observable evidence before him. The most significant fact was that Duke Albert Sovereign was extremely dead. Amy had seen a lot of dead people in her studies (and her brief career with Charlie) and the late Duke's corpse was notable on her list.

She nearly wept with relief. Then she started to

notice more. The relief was short lived. She moved to cross the barrier and a detective raised a hand at her.

"Aye, you best keep clear now, Miss—"

"Doctor," Amy and Charlie cut him off in unison. Charlie lifted the barrier and guided her under, turning sharp eyes on the cop.

"Think he's a bit past that," the detective commented.

Charlie raised an eyebrow at him, but the detective was nonplussed. He registered Amy's medical bag with a flicker of surprise. She donned her medical gloves and ignored him as she approached Sovereign's body.

"Oh aye?" he gave them a funny look. "Sorry, doc. Ya not our usual—"

"Coroner, no," Charlie agreed. "Doctor Florin is my coroner."

"The Doc Florin?" the detective eyed them both up. "That guard said youse was about. That makes you Charles Shilling? Really? Can't be. Ya—"

"Shorter than you expected," Charlie sighed.

"Oh, you do do tha thing," the detective chuckled. "'Ow'd you know I was gonna say that?"

"Everyone does," Charlie sighed. He still had his head cocked to the side, watching Amy begin her inspection. The detective stayed watching him, and both men only averted their attention as a new person sashayed around the corner. How Denarius had talked her way into the crime scene was anyone's guess, but she was a master criminal.

Amy was very carefully inspecting the body. She tried to keep as much of herself between the victim and the audience as possible. Even she felt strangely empty considering the dead man at her feet. She wanted to feel vindicated, or at least satisfied, but she still just felt afraid. She knew what she was looking for and she found it all too easily.

"I'm going to need to speak to Rory Sovereign," Charlie announced.

"We've got 'im inside for questionin' already," the detective replied. "I think we can universally agree this couldn't 'ave happened t' a nicer bloke, but it's 'ard to believe he just happened t' jump out a window while Rory was in town."

"We'll see," Charlie commented. "In the meantime, I need to speak with him, and Florin needs to examine the scene. Please do your best to see that she's undisturbed — especially when your own doctor shows up."

Amy looked for him to catch his eye, but he didn't glance her way before he vanished off inside. Instead, she caught a brief look from the detective, and then watched him lock gazes with her mother.

"He always like that?" the detective asked.

"Always," Elizabeth practically purred. "You read the papers, Inspector? You know my daughter has interesting taste in men."

Amy barely managed to refrain from directing an obscene gesture her way, but she was too preoccupied to let her mother get on her nerves. One of the first things she had noticed was a wound that did not align with fall trauma. Just as she had suspected, Sovereign had been stabbed before he had fallen out the window.

The dagger was still in his body. He had fallen on it and hidden it from immediate view. Amy knew it was there now, but exposing it incriminated someone with certainty.

Someone who didn't deserve to be incriminated. Having met the man, Amy wouldn't have judged anyone for doing what they had. Especially not the actual killer. Her heart was thumping against her ribs like it was trying to escape her body. She kept the blade carefully hidden as she turned the body to better inspect the wound. Angle, force, height… she knew exactly who had done this. She was certain. And in that moment, she made a decision. The only one she could make.

Being as careful as she could to look busy and not get caught, she slipped the dagger from the body into her medical bag and out of sight of everyone. No one ever had to know. How she was going to hide the wound from the actual coroner was another mystery entirely, but without a murder weapon to link it to, maybe they stood some kind of chance.

She realised, as she carefully began to pack up and remove her gloves, that she was deliberately trying to help someone get away with murder. She was hoping for outright dismissal, and failing that some kind of technicality. What had the DI said before? Couldn't have happened to a nicer bloke. Maybe, just maybe, the cops around here wouldn't be looking too hard.

Unless they really wanted to get Julian.

"That was quick," the detective commented to her as she came back to their side of the cordon.

"He fell the entire length of the tower," Amy pointed out. "A lot of it is self-explanatory." She took a deep, shaky breath. Her heart was still hammering. She wondered if any credit could be given to the shock of Sovereign's grizzly death, or if it was entirely her own complicity in the crime. "I would like to speak to your coroner when they arrive. Obviously there are a great many tests we can't do here. Until then, I ought to have a word with my partner."

"Let me take you to him, dear," Elizabeth offered, holding out an arm in invitation. "We'll let this excellent detective get on with his job. I really don't think I have the stomach to keep working as your translator..."

Amy let herself be led away, but once they were safely out of earshot she muttered, "My translator?"

"If anyone asks," Elizabeth replied, guiding her back around the front and into the house, via stationed officers, "you and Shilling are absolutely brilliant, but also problematically autistic and you often need someone around to help you communicate and translate your findings into layman's terms."

Amy glared at her.

"Don't look at me like that, darling," Elizabeth warned. "It's how you got your job with him, after all."

"That is not what I do for him!" she hissed venomously. "Charlie might be an unusual mind, but he does not need to be translated. I resent the implication that he cannot communicate for himself, when you and I both know that not only is he more than capable, he is exceptional at conversing with remarkable clarity across all class barriers." Amy drew herself up indignantly and glowered. "It's not translating people always hover about him for, it's minding. Especially from the upper class trying to keep him quiet. You should know better."

They walked in silence for a moment, following directions to the drawing room the police at the door had indicated Julian was in. Eventually, Elizabeth spoke.

"I did not mean to strike a nerve," she murmured.

Amy bristled. She supposed that was an apology, but she did not much feel like accepting it. It bothered her, not just as a doctor but as a person, when people tried to make out neurological diversities as ailments that ought to be treated. There were people out there, people like Harry and his friends, who thought Charlie needed treatment. Therapy, maybe, Amy would concede, but that was mostly for coping mechanisms to deal with people like that. Charlie was rather unique, but Amy would be the first person to suggest that made him more capable, not less. It was just differently capable. He wasn't good at conventional dinner parties, but he could solve murders.

She strode into the drawing room without knocking. Perhaps she should have, but she wasn't in the mood, and it hadn't occurred to her that she would walk in on anything untoward. That was, until she entered the room and found Charlie and Julian in a very tense standoff. She wouldn't go so far as to say it was a fight, but perhaps that was being generous. She took in Charlie's frustration, Julian's anger, and what looked awfully like the last remains of the offending dress

Jamie had been forced to wear to lunch going up in flames in the fireplace behind Julian.

"Ah," she summed up the situation carefully.

"Hello again, Rory," Elizabeth commented behind her, stepping into the room and carefully shutting the door behind her.

"Julian," Amy and Charlie corrected at the same time. "Julian is his preferred name," Amy added.

"Call me Rory," Julian shrugged. "I imagine I'll be getting a lot o' that now."

"Don't do this, Swift," Charlie implored.

"It's already done," Julian replied, turning to the fire with the poker and making sure the last of the bloodied dress crumbled to ash.

"The police are going to come after you, Julian," Charlie beseeched. "You're who they want for this, but the evidence—"

"Is gone," Julian cut him off sharply. "It's already done, Sleuth, an' I beg ya, keep ya nose clean o' this one. The coppers can hound me… that's fine." He turned to them, eyes black as coal. "They can learn t' fear me like they feared mah Da."

"I don't want that for you," Charlie insisted, stepping closer to his friend.

"Too bad, Sleuth," Julian sighed. "This world is fulla bad things happenin' t' good people. Ya should be used t' that by now."

"What about Skipp?" Charlie implored. "Swift… you love him—"

"You think this isn't for 'im?" Julian retorted. "You think I'm no' thinkin' of 'im every Goddamn minute,

Charlie? I have t' protect mah family. I can't just run away from this. Not this time. Mike would get that. If he were here, he'd support me."

"Of course he would, Swift. But not like this. You're not like this, Julian," Charlie insisted. "Acting like your father to get away with murder isn't the answer."

"Well, we don't all get a secret special pardon from the Lord Chief Justice for our crimes," Julian snapped.

"Julian!" Amy snapped back.

"Don't get involved, Amy," Julian warned. "I love ya, Doc, but stay outta this one."

"She's already neck deep in it," Elizabeth warned, carefully checking the door again and turning to the room. They were all watching her. The look she returned was far more calculating and shrewd than theirs. "Amy, darling, I want you to hand over whatever you just nicked from the crime scene."

"What?!" both the men barely suppressed their explosions.

Amy wanted to ask how she knew. She wanted to hold power and make demands, but, if nothing else, her mother was a world class thief. A master at her art. Of course she would have noticed Amy stealing from the crime scene. Very reluctantly, and looking around surreptitiously despite them all being alone in the room, Amy pulled out the bloody dagger she had carefully hidden in a clean bandage inside her medical bag. Denarius took it from her, careful to only touch the bandage, and wrapped it safely away in her own handbag.

"Very good, dear," Liz complimented her.

"Is that…?" Julian began.

"I had to!" Amy blurted softly. "It's the dagger Jamie used to stab him. He'd fallen on the weapon and no one seemed to have seen it yet! I had to take it, otherwise it would have incriminated Jamie!"

Very abruptly, she was whisked into Julian's arms. He squeezed her tightly, pressing her to his body. Once upon a time, Amy was confident she would have swooned to be held like this by Julian. He was very handsome and he smelled very good and he was universally charming, but knowing him like she did now, the appeal had worn into something platonic. When she hugged him back, burying her face in his shoulder, all she could think about was small, scared Jamie, and how she would do anything she could to help Julian be the father that boy actually deserved. Julian kissed her cheek as he let her go.

"Ya an angel, love," he sighed. "Thank you."

"Of course," Amy nodded, trying not to look at Charlie and the way he looked like he was about to flip the furniture. She could almost see the vein throbbing in his temple as his allies systematically destroyed the evidence of the crime.

"My next question," Denarius interrupted carefully, refusing to let them forget about her in the midst of their drama, "is how come you two get to speak privately while the police wait outside?"

"Because they think Charlie's on their side," Julian replied, stepping away from Amy and looking back at his tense friend. "They think the great sleuth is here t' help them solve a sticky case, but I've got 'im now. I love ya, Sleuth. I know ya'd never just betray me, but ya can't help wantin' t' tell the truth. It's a great shame, ya a damn good liar, but it hurts ya t' do it. Ya want the truth t' come out, it's why ya do what ya do, and ya might have tried t' get the truth out with this, but ya won't if Amy is involved. Ya'll help me lie t' protect her."

Charlie did not look like he was going to disagree… but he looked like he begrudged them everything.

"Hm," Denarius made a small, contemplative sound. "Just so I understand… Rory's little brother killed the Duke, his abusive father, and you two are covering it up to make it look like Rory did it?"

"If ya looking to blackmail—" Julian began venomously.

"Oh, never, Your Grace," Elizabeth purred. "I wouldn't dream of it. Mister Shilling, could I please have a word — *privately*?"

Amy wanted to have a heart attack, but she couldn't will one and she couldn't think of an excuse to stop them either. Charlie didn't say anything. He looked like he was trying to solve *Goldbach's Conjecture* and the furrow in his brow only intensified as he gave a slight nod and followed her from the room. Julian placed a reassuring hand on Amy's shoulder, but it did nothing.

They weren't gone for long. A few tense minutes, tempered only by Julian's undying gratitude, were soon alleviated by Charlie and Elizabeth's return. He hadn't changed at all. He still looked like he was wrestling with an impossible puzzle and there were no clues as to their discussion. None save the rather smug look on her mother's face that made Amy want to punch out a wall.

"Right then," Denarius announced. "Very carefully and quietly, children, you're going to make sure that all the properly incriminating evidence is either destroyed or in my possession. Discreetly, but with some haste, yes?"

Amy and Julian both looked to Charlie. He glowered, but gave a small, curt nod.

"Wait, what's goin' on?" Julian demanded.

"My daughter is tangled up in the crime of your father's death, Your Grace," Elizabeth smiled at him. "So I'm going to make it disappear."

"You can't just make a body disappear," Amy replied. "Everyone's already seen it. The police are investigating it."

"I'm not getting rid of the body, darling," Liz countered. "I'm getting rid of the murder. Now, is there anything else I need to have or know about before I go?"

The question hung in the air. Charlie managed to ease his glare long enough to cock a questioning eyebrow at Julian. He shook his head.

"Very good," Elizabeth smiled. "Destroy anything else you find. I'll be back when I'm done."

She turned and left without another word. Amy stared after her, but realised after a moment she was just looking at a closed door. Still, she couldn't tear her eyes away. The only thing that finally forced it was the sound of Charlie's deep and frustrated sigh.

"The house staff will all alibi themselves," he commented. "Julian, if there is any possible way to have you, Jamie, and Anne alibi each other without reneging previous alibis, and while maintaining plausible deniability of the incident, you need to see to that."

Julian nodded slowly.

"That hardest thing will be the coroner…" Amy murmured. "I… I can try and hide the stab wound —"

"And the poison?" Charlie grimaced, rubbing his tired eyes.

Amy and Julian both stared at him. It took him a moment to realise they were looking. It did not improve his mood.

"Yes, he was poisoned before he was stabbed and thrown out the window," Charlie glowered.

"How can you possibly…?" Amy murmured. The look he shot her in response made her want to slap him. "Charlie! That is infuriating! How do you do that?! How can you possibly know that?!"

"How can you not?!" he retorted. "You're the doctor! You're the bloody doctor, Amelia, how did you miss it?! You panicked, and now we're leaving it to someone for whom the extent of my trust wouldn't fill a teaspoon. We don't worry about the coroner, we worry about aligning our lies."

"I didn't panic," Amy snapped. "I haven't had the time or resources to do any toxin tests —"

"I didn't test for it," Charlie stated. "The foam and discolouration around his mouth didn't come from the fall and it would not have manifested the way it had post-mortem."

Amy froze. She hadn't noticed that. The sudden realisation that it had been staring her in the face and she'd missed it was cutting.

"The bastard fell so far he's 'alf jelly," Julian commented in her defence. "Who's lookin' at 'is mouth?"

"Anyone investigating why he fell," Charlie growled. He looked to Amy but she couldn't meet his eye. She'd messed up and she knew it, but his tone wasn't quite so vicious when he spoke again. "Everyone looking at that body is looking for a crime. You saw the second one, the one you were afraid of finding, and it made you panic, which made you miss the initial crime."

"Well, what about you?" she muttered. "The way you took off up the drive... you can't tell me you weren't panicking about Julian."

"I'll concede that," Charlie muttered. "But the instant I saw the body, I knew Julian hadn't done it. No offense, Swift, but if you'd killed your father, it would not have looked like that."

"Aye," Julian nodded. "Agreed."

"Next you're going to tell me you knew it was Duke Sovereign who'd died before you saw him too," Amy muttered.

The look Charlie gave her very nearly made her want to murder him. Unique mind indeed. She hoped he knew she was now as angry with him as he was with her, even if his anger was logically justified and hers was personal.

"Of course," Charlie stared at her like everything was obvious. "If Sovereign had still been alive, the staff would not have been gathered with the police the way they were. He had to have been the victim. Like everyone else, I assumed Julian had finally cracked, until I saw what had been done to the Duke. Unfortunately, no one else seems to be able to keep up. The deduction of the order of events is not hard, if you actually pay attention."

Amy shared a look with Julian. Sometimes, it was hard to remember why they both loved their scruffy and obnoxious little companion.

"And my mother convinced you to help us cover it up?" Amy muttered.

"It's what the aristocracy deserves," Charlie shrugged. "They spend their entire lives lying about their entitlement, as through any human is more or less deserving than another, why not let them die entombed in lies as well?"

"That's the Sleuth I know an' love," Julian approved, pulling Charlie into a one-armed hug and kissing the top of his messy hair. "Come on, Charlie. Come help us commit crimes for a change, instead o' solving them. I bet ya bloody good at it."

"Unparalleled," Charlie sighed reluctantly.

Amy followed behind as Julian led Charlie off to his family's 'interrogation'. She watched him closely. It would be a lie to pretend she wasn't always watching him closely. Half of what she'd learnt of his observation had come from watching him. She was furious with herself for missing such obvious clues. He was right, she'd been too worried about Jamie to see the whole picture. Now… now she was trying to see the whole picture and she was worried about Charlie.

Once there had been a time when nothing could keep

him from justice. Not even Harry. He had forced the truth into the daylight then, no matter what it had done to either of them or anyone else. He had been determined to bring the Jack to justice, and his morals would not let him stoop to vengeance to achieve it. Then had come Argent and Balles, and Charlie had swallowed his morals for her. He had let Argent get away with murder, for her.

Then had come Kopeck and the gruesome death of poor Esther. Amy had been shot. Then Kopeck had been... removed. She could still hear Charlie's voice across the sheets in the dark as he told her he didn't even feel bad about it. Stubborn, virtuous Charlie Shilling... he'd become everything he swore to stop, and he said it didn't bother him... but she could see it. She could see it eating him alive even if he couldn't...

And now there was this. The murder of Duke Sovereign, deserved or not, and Charlie was helping her cover it up. She hadn't asked. She had just acted, and it had been right and just and full of pure intentions, and now Charlie was committing more crimes. For her. Even Elizabeth Denarius had known how to exploit that. She was going to have to do something about it.

12

Charlie had coached the Sovereigns and stonewalled the police. That had been his job from Denarius and he had done it expertly. None of it gave him any satisfaction. Not sitting with Anne, quietly and privately while the Sovereign brothers talked, and informing her that she was free. The first to crack and the last to be caught. No one was ever going to know what she did, and Julian was going to cover for Jamie if Denarius' plan failed.

That had helped the Duchess turn on genuine waterworks for the interrogation. The police didn't have to know she was crying from relief. Even if they did, who would blame her? Seeing the new and tentative hope in Anne and Jamie should have soothed Charlie's soul. It didn't. Not enough. Not really.

The coroner wasn't going to get their report in until morning. Charlie insisted on spending the night with Julian this time. At the very least, he could help the new Duke Sovereign get his affairs in order. He couldn't bear the thought of another night at The Shephard's Arms. Not after the last one.

Amy opted to retrieve their things in order to stay with Jamie and Anne. Charlie had been rather precious about Julian insisting he send someone for their effects. Fortunately, his friends knew how to be patient with him, and Amy retrieving their things was an acceptable compromise. Now that Julian was in charge and Charlie was allowed to fight the system without putting more lives in danger, he had opinions on servitude again.

Julian was prepared to humour him, although both of them knew it was mostly formality. He was going over the legality of his father's will with a fine-toothed comb. They had already identified the necessary loopholes.

In the large, stained-oak panelled drawing room, with the curtains drawn against the night and the roaring fire devouring any last shreds of evidence, Julian sat back in his chair and put his feet up with a sigh.

"Can't believe the bastard got what he always wanted..." he mused.

"He wanted his son to try and kill him," Charlie acknowledged. "I wonder if he was proud..."

"I know I am," Julian grinned.

Charlie didn't smile back. Even the death of someone as horrible as Sovereign was still a horrible death. He wanted it to be satisfying. He wanted it to be righteous. He wanted it to make him feel the way he'd felt killing Kopeck, like he was doing God's work. An instrument of her divine will.

All it did was make him realise that had been an illusion too. Everyone knew he'd done it. Julian had shoved it in his face multiple times since they'd been here, jealously wishing he could have used the same legal shield to remove his father. Now Charlie just knew all he'd done was gotten away with murder. It wasn't divine. It was just state sanctioned. He'd carried out capital punishment… two days early.

"You're troubled," Julian warned him. His accent changed and it felt for a moment like Charlie was talking to his old friend again. He looked back. Julian wasn't smiling anymore. He was eyeing Charlie knowingly.

"Is that surprising?" he asked.

"Na, just concernin'," Julian shook his head. He took his feet off the desk and patted the seat next to him. Charlie crossed the room and sat in the offered chair. "Wanna tell me what's goin' on?"

"So many things…" Charlie sighed, fidgeting with his ring.

"Then let's start with what's goin' on with Amy," Julian suggested.

"Hm," Charlie frowned. "She missed things today. Obvious things she wouldn't normally have missed. I think Sovereign's treatment of Jamie upset her deeply. She wasn't thinking clearly."

"As much as I would love t' blame the old cock for everythin' wrong with the world," Julian replied. "I really think that it might not've been Jamie messing with her head. I imagine she had plenty bangin' around in her brain to distract her — like her concern for you after ya panic attack last night."

Charlie blushed. He should have known Amy would tell Julian about that, but he really wished she hadn't. Some things should be allowed to stay private. He shook his head to himself, staring down at the signet ring he was twisting around his finger.

"She told me she was in love with me…" he muttered.

"That's nice," Julian replied knowingly. "It's not why ya had a panic attack though."

Charlie blushed harder. It was warm in here with the fire going. Too warm. The feeling of Amy's hands on him was like the ghost of a memory creeping back to haunt him. It was so hot. He needed to strip off some layers, but he was too nervous to move.

"I don't want to talk about it," he muttered.

"That's fine," Julian told him. "Ya don't 'ave t' talk t' me. Ya are gonna 'ave t' talk t' her though, at some stage."

Charlie made a reluctant sound, and Julian chuckled at him. He understood, but he begrudged it a little.

"Ya used t' give me and Skipp such a 'ard time…" Julian reminded. "Think of it as returnin' the favour."

"But…" Charlie started weakly and then realised he didn't have the rest of the sentence.

"Ya love her, Charlie," Julian said. "Ya love her easily as much as she loves you, and the two o' ya are perfect for each other. It's just the same. Every reason I used with ya t' defend mah distance with Skipp seemed reasonable at the time. Now it just seems petty, lookin' back. A waste. I love 'im. I shouldn't ever 'ave pretended anythin' else. There's isn't anythin' I wouldn't do for that man, includin' comin' up 'ere and killin' mah Da — which I didn't do, but I woulda. Talk t' her, Charlie. Tell 'er what's going on with ya."

Charlie nodded reluctantly. It wasn't a guarantee, but it was what he needed to get Swift off his back. Besides, his friend had a point.

The next morning moved by in a strange wave of abnormality. No one was quite sure what to do with themselves. The Estate was oddly calm without Albert Sovereign. Everyone was sleeping easier, but the small tics and nerves of residual trauma would linger for years, and the guilt was palpable. Everyone knew, or at the very least suspected, what had happened. No one said a word.

The family were trying to pretend nothing had happened, but that was impossible with the demon that had hung over them abruptly gone. They didn't know what life without him looked like — what it was allowed to look like. Anne and Jamie moved about the house like they still expected to be set upon by a ghost. There was tentative hope. The smallest glimmer. It would take a long time to get over what had been done to them, but at least now there was space to grow. To heal.

The staff did not seem overly upset by the loss of their brutal master. Most of them probably just wanted to keep their jobs, and everyone seemed curious about Rory. What would he be like as the new Duke? Best to stay on his good side until they could find out.

Charlie was quickly bored of watching it unfold, but

he couldn't leave. They needed to know what was going to happen next. He needed to wait for Elizabeth Denarius.

Elizabeth Florin.

He could not help but use that name for her in the quiet parts of his brain. She was a Florin. She was Florin's mother, and therefore an extension of Florin. Whom he was not speaking to. Again.

This time she wasn't pushing it. He knew she was angry with him for the way things had unfolded over Sovereign's death yesterday. She had that look in her eye. That skillet-hitting look. One day she was going to do it too. He wondered if that was going to be how he died, whacked over the head with a skillet by Florin. The real question would be if he deserved it.

By midmorning, Julian had noticed his agitation and decided to head off the problem in a most agreeable fashion. That meant that the two of them were throwing clay in a studio overlooking the stank in the eastern courtyard, and the rather large black fish that dwelt within, when Elizabeth whatever-her-name-was returned. She was shown through to them by the butler, who instantly agreed to fetch the others at Julian's request.

"Yes, I quite agree the family should be around for this," Elizabeth agreed, eyeing them both up with notable surprise.

Charlie glanced at Julian for further clarification, but Julian wasn't looking at him. He was eyeing Elizabeth, looking for some hint as to whether the news was good or bad. The fact that the police weren't back at their door was promising, but given Elizabeth's entanglement in the case anything could be about to happen.

The two potters were still up to their wrists in mud, but Charlie was loath to stop if talks were about to be had. His brain worked better when his hands were busy, and it was altogether possible that he was going to need his brain. Elizabeth was still eyeing him up. He lifted an eyebrow in enquiry at her notable curiosity.

"You're not as scrawny as I thought, Mister Shilling…" she commented.

Julian snorted. Charlie looked between them in confusion, but no one seemed prepared to elaborate. An echoing voice projected down the corridor.

"We do not ogle the gentlemen, mother!" Florin called, guiding Anne and Jamie into the room.

Anne walked like a woman constantly on the verge of flinching, and Jamie hung around her like an anxious limpet. Amy stood by them protectively. It was admirable. In time, hopefully, they wouldn't need it, but it was good they had someone strong supporting them now.

"I'm sure his Grace doesn't mind a little bit of ogling…" Elizabeth chuckled.

"In mah line o' work I'm used t' it, but eyeing the son-in-law's a bit odd, don't ya think?" Julian replied.

It took Charlie entirely too long to get the joke, and he only deduced it in the end because he could read the discomfort of both Florin women. The sticking point for him being, quite obviously, that he and Florin were not even romantically involved, let alone married. He knew, unequivocally, that if he said that aloud someone would hit him. So he stayed silent.

"Hardly necessary," Elizabeth rebuked Julian's comment and tapped his bare shoulder with a rolled up newspaper.

"Is that the one with Da's death in it?" Jamie asked softly, eyes fixed on the paper.

Everyone looked to the anxious boy. He was loitering between Amy and Anne, his small hands gripping his mother's sleeve like he was scared he was about to be dragged away.

"It mentions it," Elizabeth nodded. "It's this morning's paper."

"Sovereign died, investigation ongoin', survived by wife and two children," Julian rattled off.

Elizabeth nodded. "That's what the paper says, but things have evolved since then. The investigation should be wrapping up as we speak, and I expect you'll hear from the police again this afternoon."

"Meanin'?" Julian glowered at having to coax more out of her.

"Meaning the coroner ruled Sovereign's death an accident," Elizabeth smirked. "The old man was drunk and fell out the window."

Silence reigned.

"You're welcome, by the way," she added.

Charlie wanted to ask how she'd swung that, and then decided he didn't want to know. He had studied her methods long enough to appreciate that any of the usual seductive, blackmail, thievery, or general criminal tactics could have come into play. He didn't need to know which she had employed.

The first person to move or speak was Amy. She flew across the room and threw her arms around Elizabeth. Her mother was startled at first, but her surprise quickly dissolved into pleasure as she embraced her daughter back.

"Thank you," Amy gushed.

"Of course, darling," Elizabeth squeezed her, looking across the room and meeting Anne's eye with a soft and knowing look. "Any mother would have done the same."

"So that's it then?" Charlie stood carefully from his pottery wheel, using his forearm to push the hair out of his eyes. "It's over?"

There was something about it all that felt too simple. Too clean. Far, far too easy. Nothing in his life was that easy. There had to be another shoe waiting to drop.

"It's as over as you can let it be," Elizabeth told him archly. There was a challenge in that stance. A question. She wasn't certain he could do it. She had done her part, delivered everything she'd promised. But he was still the part of it she didn't trust, just like she had been the part he didn't trust. She thought he would crack beneath the lie. Too easy indeed.

It was over. Quite the drama, but surprisingly minimal hassle. Everyone had talked it over and, once the police had come by to confirm Elizabeth's story and offer their condolences, it was done. There was no reason to stay.

Not really. Part of Amy wanted to stay and help look after Jamie and Anne for a bit, but she understood that it was going to be nice for them to have their own space to grow into for a while. She had promised to write. Part of her wanted to spend time with her mother… but she wasn't sure how quickly that could become overwhelming. So they decided to spend a test afternoon together, and Amy scheduled herself to get the overnight train back to London with Charlie and Julian.

Julian had made quite the point of organising things for his family. Anne had apologised profusely to him with her heart on her sleeve. She knew he never wanted this and, if he needed to abdicate, she understood, even if abdicating would leave her and Jamie without a home. Julian didn't believe in such nonsense. He did believe in sticking it to his father as thoroughly as possible beyond the grave. That meant he was happy to take over (legally speaking), but he needed her to take care of everything for a couple of weeks while he sorted his own business in London. Then, in two weeks, he would need her and Jamie to come to London for his wedding. And after his wedding he might need her to manage things a bit longer for… an undisclosed length of time that they could confirm later… and once Jamie was old enough to be legally recognised then Julian could abdicate — with an elaborate flourish, they were sure.

Amy was pleased for them. It was the kind of happy ending she would have wished for their family. They deserved it after everything they had been through.

Now she was just left deciding what her own happy ending should look like. It didn't feel certain. Nothing was. But she was wandering the gardens of the Sovereign Estate arm-in-arm with her mother, something she wouldn't have believed possible yesterday, and that was something.

"Do… do you think you'll be able to come and visit me in London?" Amy asked hesitantly.

"I will make a point of it, if you would like me to," Elizabeth smiled.

"You're not going to get in trouble?" Amy checked. "With the Law? With old marks? With—"

"Darling, getting oneself in trouble is half the fun of living," Elizabeth laughed. "Speaking of which—"

"Oh no," Amy shook her head.

"Speaking of which," Elizabeth repeated firmly, jiggling her grip on Amy's elbow. "What exactly is going on with you and Shilling? I do not remember this tension last time we met."

"Last time you two met you were locked in a tower and I imagine you had other things on your mind," Amy pointed out.

"Quite," Liz agreed. "However, that boy was prepared to lie, cheat, steal, and break me out to protect you. I've been around the block enough times in my life to know that's not nothing. He was not okay back then, and he's not okay now, but it's a different kind of not okay."

"A lot's changed since then…" Amy admitted, thinking about how strange it was that so much had happened in so short a time period. She felt like she had squeezed a lot of life into her days since meeting Charlie. Maybe that was just what life with him was like. Maybe that was why he was so exciting. "Actually," she blurted, unable to stop herself, "I'm worried about him."

"How so?" Liz inquired.

Amy thought about it. She didn't know how much to tell her. She couldn't tell her everything. She couldn't mention Kopeck. But… she could mention…

"Charlie and I…" she began slowly. "We… well, things got a little steamy between us the other night…"

Liz laughed. "You sound surprised, sweetheart."

"They didn't stay steamy," Amy huffed. "He had a panic attack."

Liz stopped laughing and considered Amy carefully. Once she knew she wasn't about to be teased again, Amy began the weighty process of elaborating.

"We were getting on rather well," she admitted. "But… he… things stopped very abruptly. I didn't even realise what had happened at first. Then I found him hyperventilating on the floor."

"Oh, he was properly…?" Liz commented.

"Properly panicking," Amy agreed. "I talked to Julian about it. He hinted that Charlie might have been assaulted as an adolescent and coping all these years by burying it."

Elizabeth didn't say anything. Her expression was grimly thoughtful and her arm stayed firmly linked in Amy's. They strolled slowly across the lawns in the rose garden, although it was not the season for flowers. Somehow, the naked thorny brambles felt appropriate.

The fountain in the centre wasn't running, and the water sitting in the bottom was cold and dark. Amy let the silence sit between them for a while, but eventually she felt the need to break it.

"What do I do?" she asked softly.

"You want my advice?" Liz raised an eyebrow at her.

Amy didn't know what to say. She swallowed timidly. No one needed to point out to her that her mother was probably not the best person to speak to for relationship advice, but she was who Amy had right now, and she was still her mother. A girl should be able to talk to her mother about this sort of thing. Elizabeth seemed to understand that, even if it wasn't spoken. Her eyes were full of patience and sympathy.

"Give him some space, but don't abandon him," she answered finally. "Talk to him, if you can. Communication is the key to any lasting relationship, be it romantic or otherwise. Charlie Shilling... he's a good sort, darling. He loves you. If you love him too, don't let him get away. Just make sure he has room to breathe. You're not like me, Amelia, you won't walk the path I did. You and Charlie... you just need a bit of patience — and some more confidence in this area. I understand that after everything you two have been through, matters of the heart must be a tender area, but... all wounds heal, Amelia. In time. Trust me. If I were you... I would risk this."

"If you were me?" Amy echoed.

"Well, I think we both know I never risked it for me, so feel free to take my advice with a grain of salt," Liz sighed. "Lasting monogamy was never on the cards for me. I'm not the type. You, darling, I think are very much the type. Some people are. Charlie is special to you, isn't he?"

"Yes," Amy admitted, not for the first time.

"Then don't let him slip away, love," Liz advised. "Help him, but don't push him." Elizabeth smiled and gave a soft breath of a chuckle. She patted Amy's hand lovingly. "You're a doctor, darling, you're much smarter and more knowledgeable about such things than I am. I'm sure you'll be fine."

It was the kind of charm Amy was certain her mother used to swindle everyone she met, but the crazy thing was, it worked. She didn't even care if she was getting swindled. It felt real. It felt like faith — like a mother's love — and it was exactly what she needed.

13

Charlie was pleased to see the back of Edinburgh. He didn't have anything against the city personally. In fact, he'd had plenty of good experiences there and in Scotland in general. His first trip had been with Rebecca and their father with he was five. Those were only good memories. He worried that this trip had no good memories, and he wouldn't be able to forget them.

The others had said their farewells at the Estate, which made the trip to the station and catching of the train nice and simple. Charlie appreciated nice and simple at the moment. He would take the wins he could get. The three of them had a rather lavish four-bunk cabin booked. Julian had taken the opportunity to splurge with his newfound wealth, before his stepmother began to responsibly reign him in. Charlie didn't have it in him to fight Julian on the evils of aristocracy and greed. Right now, Julian deserved this, and Charlie needed it.

Darkness had fallen by the time they were on board and only the small lamps of the cabin lit the room. The three of them sat around on the lower bunks, chatting and gossiping. Well, mostly Julian and Amy, but Charlie joined in where he could. Mostly he just liked listening to them. He was sitting on the end of Amy's bunk, leaning against the wall. She was up the other end with a safe distance between them. Julian was on his own bed across from them, looking strangely comfortable for someone who had just successfully covered up a murder. Perhaps not strangely, given the circumstances. He had lost his accent almost as soon as the train started moving, like he was free from home and slipping back into the persona of Julian Silver.

"I have a question for you two," he announced.

"Hm?" Amy encouraged him sleepily, nesting on her pillows.

"When we get back, I'm serious about this wedding," he began.

"No one doubted that, Swift," Charlie smiled wryly.

Julian smirked at him. "I want you two to be my groomsmen, if you'd be willing?"

"Of course!" Amy exclaimed. "Julian, we'd be delighted."

"You asked Jamie to be your Best Man?" Charlie checked.

Julian shared a look with Amy. "You're right, it's infuriating when he does that."

"Oh, come on!" Charlie protested.

"That was a perfectly logical conclusion, Julian," Amy smiled. "But I know what you mean. He's the only one that gets to have secrets…"

"I am not," Charlie huffed, feeling an awful lot like his own business had been dragged in front of too many people recently. "You two have plenty, I'm sure."

"Like what?" Julian laughed.

"I wouldn't know," Charlie sniffed. "They're secrets."

Julian and Amy were both laughing, and he was fairly confident they were laughing at him, but he let them have that one. Instead, he sat back on the bed and pulled out a book from his bag. However comfortable their carriage was, enclosed spaces with other people were not his preference. The distraction was essential, and it carried him through the trip until he was appropriately sleepy. He wasn't sure how much time he lost inside it.

"An Alice Jones?" Amy commented, peering at the cover as she sidled up to him. "I haven't read that one."

"It's new," Charlie replied, noting that Julian had given up and gone to sleep, which meant he was now taking up her space if she wanted to sleep. "I think everyone's so concerned with the new Florence Pound that it perhaps got a bit missed," he smiled shyly at her. "You can borrow it when I'm done."

"I'd like that," she smiled. Somehow, abruptly, she was sitting with him, her shoulder pressed to his and the scent of her perfume no longer soothing to his senses. He wondered when that had changed. If he should blame the other night, or if perhaps, a night further back, when her scents of soft lavender and rose had mixed with the scents of blood and ash... and something irreversibly toxic had been born in him.

"Florin..." he whispered, barely above the noise of the train.

"Amy," she corrected him.

He looked to her. In the dim light of their cabin she

was a shadowy figure at his side, even her hair looked dark. He had been hunched over his book with his knees up, struggling to read in the near dark. Now it felt like he was scrunched up protectively, and he didn't know how to untie himself. But she was looking at him with patience. It was firm and confident, but it was still patience.

"Whatever you have to say, Charlie, I'll hear it," she told him. "But I want you to use my name, my given name, like we're friends."

"We are friends…" he whispered.

"Then please treat me like one," she implored. "Please, Charlie."

He nodded, but he couldn't look at her anymore. His chest was tight and his throat was constricted. He couldn't breathe properly. It felt like the night before. It was building. He sat there for a moment, staring at the dark window, watching nothing but the night outside. He couldn't even see his reflection from this angle. He focused on his breathing, forcing himself to take long slow breaths and hold them.

"Julian… told me I needed to talk to you…" he whispered once he could force words out.

She placed a hand on his arm and patted him gently.

"That would be nice," she replied. "But it doesn't have to be here, and it doesn't have to be now."

Charlie buried his face in his book. The paper was cold against his skin, and it was safe and dark in there, and no one could look at him. He breathed on the pages and inhaled their inky smell.

"We are friends, Amy," he whispered to the book,

trying to force himself to do better. She needed this. She deserved it. It shouldn't be so hard to give. But he couldn't think... he couldn't think past the wall that sheltered him from his own memories.

Her hand slid from his arm and up around his shoulders. It was comforting and affectionate. She placed a tender kiss at his temple. It asked nothing of him. He squeezed his eyes shut, fighting back tears. He didn't want to get the pages wet. His breath was trembling against the paper.

"You're okay, Charlie," she whispered. Her hand rubbed his back gently. "Just breathe, Charlie. Just breathe. You're okay."

He nodded, his hair scrunching against the paper. The sound was mostly lost in the rumble of the train.

"I've got you," she promised. "I've got you, Charlie, and I don't need anything from you right now. Whatever else we are, Charlie, whatever that is or might one day be... all I want for now... is... is just to be your safe space. I want you to know that, whatever else, you'll always be safe with me."

He felt like he should be weeping. He was worried that he might have gotten tears on the book. But his face felt dry even though his eyes stung, and his breathing was coming easier. Her hand on his hunched back, making small circles over his spine, was incredibly soothing.

"I know Scotland was hard," she whispered. "I know we both... we opened a Pandora's box or two. It's starting to feel like we can't catch a break. I know... I know we're both angry. What happened with the

Sovereigns... Charlie, I know I'm not alone in being angry about that. It isn't fair, but I think we're both angry at ourselves and each other for that. I know your anger about what happened is logically justified and mine is just personal—"

He laughed and she stopped talking. He hadn't meant to laugh, and he heard the tears in his own laughter. Breathing was definitely easier now, and he was able to raise his head from the book again. He folded it closed and set it aside with a deep breath. His eyes stayed closed. He knew he'd cry if he opened them.

"You think mine isn't personal?" he smiled softly in the darkness. "Really, Amy? You think it isn't? The only reason I cared at all is because I was worried about you. I didn't want anything to happen you, and I was scared I'd dragged you into another mess that put you in danger. It doesn't get more personal than that."

She didn't say anything but he could feel her eyes staring at him in the dark. She kissed his cheek. He wanted to turn into it. He wanted to turn his lips to hers and draw her to him in the dark, but he knew he'd start to panic again. He wished he wouldn't, but he couldn't seem to make it stop. The only way to resist was to remove himself from the situation.

"Thank you, Amy," he whispered, resting his head against her shoulder for a moment. "I think I'm going to go to bed and let you be."

"Sleep well, Charlie," she replied, her fingers brushing against his face. "I'll be here if you need me."

He left her side, immediately aware of the cold in her absence. It was always cold in her absence. He didn't open his eyes until he was standing and facing his bunk, and even then he only opened them to clamber up onto the bed above. Amy waited until he was safely up and settled before she extinguished the last light. He wondered if she'd ever know the strength it had taken him to walk away from her then. He wondered if it would have been worth the panic attack. The thought wasn't enough to make him go back down, but he lay awake in the dark, comforted by the rattle and sway of the train, and thought of her.

The morning was proper London dreary when they arrived back and all three of them were grateful for it. The thin and miserable rain was appropriately melancholy and cleansing. While all of them were eager to be home, they had a more pressing matter to attend to. Amy enjoyed the surprise on Julian's face as they arrived at her friends' front door.

Jane and Laura had been living together since medical school, in a townhouse that belonged to the Mark family. It was new money and as such was appropriately ostentatious. Amy knew Charlie hated it. He had, however, put his personal feelings aside for the wellbeing of his friend. Something she was all too aware was a standard activity for him.

As glad as she was to see her friends again, and as grateful as she was to them for treating and hiding Michael in their home, it was nothing like Julian's reaction. Amy was almost jealous as everyone was kissed and Michael, upon abandoning the many bandages of his leprosy disguise, was physically leapt upon. It took almost no time for Amy and Charlie to decide they needed to get the boys out of Laura and Jane's house before Julian publicly started something they would all regret. Laura and Jane were less convinced, but Amy truly couldn't tell if they were genuinely curious or just messing with everyone.

Either way, it would be good to get Michael and Julian home and put the entire case behind them. Charlie offered to her that she stay with her friends, and she was half tempted, until Laura started telling her about this new Dawson & Kropp novel by debut author Florence Pound and how much she would love it. The statement was followed by an implication there was a character in the book Amy might quite like, and she decided she would much rather see their charges safely home and call it a day. That was, until they got to the bakery. It hadn't occurred to her what she'd really wanted until she was staring at it, and then it was so obvious she couldn't believe it had taken so long.

She made sure Charlie was occupied with his friends and then excused herself on the grounds of exhaustion. No one questioned it. Then, once they were safely inside, she crossed the street and knocked on the door.

There were so many things stewing in her mind. There were a thousand different things she wanted to say to Jasper Quid, but when he opened the door she completely blanked on all of them. Then she punched him in the face.

Fortunately, Susan and Rebecca weren't home. Fortunately, Charlie was well occupied at the bakery and had no idea she was here. Also fortunately, Jasper's nose didn't bleed for too long. It was perhaps ten minutes after Amy had punched him in the face, and the two of them were sitting down to tea in the parlour while Amy helped Jasper hold a handkerchief to his face.

"Just… just keep your head tilted a bit longer…" she suggested.

"Thank you, Doctor," he replied, the stiffness in his voice partially muffled by the bloody handkerchief.

"I am sorry I hit you…" she apologised, although in truth she wasn't sure she was. It just seemed like the right thing to say.

Jasper seemed to know this, and stayed carefully silent. Amy took the time to consider him properly. Jasper was an unassuming man, perhaps as many as ten years older than Charlie but certainly no more. His face looked rather pale and pinched, but that could have been mostly brought on by the bloody nose.

"I must say…" he admitted, dabbing at the last of the blood, "it was rather a surprise."

"You bang him over the head often enough when he's coming through doorways," Amy retorted. "I'm almost surprised that you're surprised someone got you back."

"Is that what this is about?" He lifted an unamused eyebrow.

"No," Amy shook her head. "Not directly, anyway. Perhaps tangentially."

Jasper sniffed and looked away. "I don't know what he told you—"

"He didn't tell me anything," Amy cut him off. "He didn't say a word. He did have a panic attack while we were away though. So I talked to Julian, who'd talked to Michael… and no one knew anything. No one knew anything for sure, but there were rumours…"

"Doctor, you know better than most that Shilling has endured a remarkably trying year," Jasper snapped. "If he's having panic attacks, it's hardly surprising, but I can't imagine why you're talking to me—"

"Is it true?" Amy demanded, unable to wait politely. Jasper's attitude was twitchy and defensive. He was trying to hide something and doing it badly. "Something happened at the wedding? Is it true?"

"I don't know what he—" Jasper tried again.

"He didn't say anything, Jasper," Amy snapped. "He hasn't told a soul. Not me. Not his sisters. Not his friends. He hasn't said a word. Honestly, I think that might be more telling than anything. No wonder he does what he does for others after what you did to him."

"I did not—!" Jasper choked, strangling his own cry of outrage. He met her eyes and all the venom he had reserved when she hit him doubled down. He looked like she'd struck him now. The fear and loathing in his eyes was unbearable, seemingly to him as well because he could not hold her gaze. His voice trembled when he spoke again. "You don't understand."

"Try me," she challenged, confident that she had her answer even if she didn't have all the information. The challenge hung in the air as Jasper struggled to meet it. It took a moment for him to break, but break he did.

"He. Tricked. Me," Jasper whispered. Everything from his voice to his hands shook, and he clasped the bloody handkerchief tightly to try and keep from trembling. "I… I didn't know, Doctor. I had no idea…"

"He was fourteen!" Amy hissed at him.

Jasper released a small, choking breath, sucking his lips like he was trying to hold back insane laughter. Pained laughter. The kind of laughter someone releases when they're standing on the precipice and the only options are laugh at the agony or jump.

"So people like to remind me…" he whispered like they were his last words. Jasper shook his head, staring down at the bloody rag in his hands. "You don't understand, Doctor…" The shaking was getting worse and Jasper kept having to pause to steady his breathing. "He hasn't changed, you know. Not barely at all across the years. He was mostly the same back then. He certainly didn't look fourteen. He… he was just a young man who showed up with the rest of Lady Rebecca's guests from the High House. They came here for the final reception. I… I had no idea who he was. He was just a man from the High House."

Amy didn't say anything. It made sense, in a horrible kind of way.

"Some of the other workers… we were having a few drinks. A few couldn't hurt. It was Lady Guinea's wedding." Jasper shivered through his whole body like a ghost was passing through him. "We weren't hurting anyone…" A soft and gentle desperation wafted through Jasper's voice. "He… he came to drink with us. Said he'd rather spend time with us than the oppressive tyrants of the aristocracy. He stole wine from the wedding party. Everyone… everyone thought him so wild, so daring, but charming." He turned and looked her straight in the eye. She couldn't hide from it and it pierced her knowingly. "You know the way he can be, Doctor. You know exactly what I'm talking about. He… he pushed me to drink with him, all the while talking about overthrowing the class system and liberating the people… telling me I deserved more than what the self-appointed upper class would allow of me. He made me feel special, Doctor. That way that only Charlie can. I know you know what I mean."

She did know what he meant, and for a moment she almost felt sorry for him. It was all starting to make her feel sick, but maybe that was because she understood. She understood all too well.

"He was in my room, Doctor," Jasper whispered. "He was in my room, getting me drunk, and telling me that I deserved the world. We were both drunk. I've never been so drunk, Doctor. I'm surprised anything happened, but we were young and…" he paused. "No one—" Jasper's voice cracked. "No one had ever made me feel special like that before. I… I thought I was going to wake up to a bill. I was worried in the morning I'd be hit with a bill from the High House I couldn't afford, but… but I hoped…" Jasper squeezed his eyes shut and trailed off.

Amy closed her own eyes for a moment. She couldn't look anymore. She couldn't bear to see. It was both somehow worse and better than she'd imagined, but she couldn't weather Jasper's heartbreak. It was so real. So awful.

"You hoped you were Christ and Magdalene and you woke up with the underage little brother of your Lady's new wife…" Amy whispered. It was worse when she said it out loud. Jasper looked like he wanted to drown himself.

"He said it best we both pretend nothing ever happened," Jasper finished like he was sucking poison.

"He broke your heart," Amy concluded. "That's why you've been taking petty revenge ever since."

Jasper made a sound like he was about to protest, but Amy stood up and the action silenced him.

"Jasper, you hurt him—"

"No!" Jasper glared at her. He stared her straight in the eye with unwavering conviction. "No, you don't get to do that. He doesn't get to do that. Not after what he did to me. He gets to pretend like nothing ever happened—"

"You hurt him, Jasper!" Amy repeated, cutting him off and stepping closer, looming over him. "You want to pretend like you were the only one who was hurt because that's easier, but you weren't. He was just a boy, and something he didn't want and wasn't ready for happened to him, and he has been coping with that by burying it! You were the adult in that situation, inebriated or not, and you were wrong."

"Well, I'm sorry I didn't hear the punctuation between his gasps of 'don't' and 'stop'," Jasper spat. "You weren't there, Doctor. You don't understand. It wasn't my fault!"

"It wasn't anyone else's fault," Amy replied, her patience wearing thin at the absence of his integrity. "He was a child, Jasper, and not only did you assault him, but your response has been to bully him in his own home ever since."

"So what?" Jasper snarled at her. "I'm monstrous and evil and you're going to the police? Is that how this story ends?"

"No," Amy shook her head slowly. "Charlie never said anything. I'm not going to start something he hasn't. But if we're going to help him, if I'm going to help my friend heal, you're going to have to start answering for what you've done — one way or another."

Jasper looked like he was about to fight her, like a coiled snake preparing to strike, but she picked up her bag and walked from the house. He didn't follow and he had better sense than to call after her.

14

It was late in the evening, night had fallen properly over the city and the moon only peeked occasionally through the smoggy clouds. Charlie was in the studio. Working with Julian had been therapeutic, if only for that morning. It was good to be throwing clay again. It was good for his mind, good for his hands. He could do it again. He could craft a piece and then cut it from the wheel without seeing Kopeck. Without even thinking of her. He could use his wire for its intended purpose again. He could almost feel like himself again.

But the night had fallen dark and thick and the orange electric lamps could only do so much to hold it at bay. It wasn't good light to work by, and it was worse to keep his own darkness at bay. Perhaps he could have Julian over to work with in the daylight hours again sometime soon, once the wedding was out of the way.

He began the cleanup, setting aside his work to dry before firing, rinsing his tools in the sink. He was drying his hands when he heard it. The strange scraping from the hallway. It was an unusual sound. Something banging, clattering. Almost like —

Charlie bolted from the studio like the hounds of Hell were after him. He didn't even put down his clay knife. He crashed into the hallway at speed, finding the dim silhouette hanging from the beams in the hallway. He rushed over, tripping on the chair he'd heard hit the floor, staggering, and throwing his arms around Jasper's legs, trying to hold him up.

"Don't you dare!" he ordered, like it would make a bit of difference. Charlie knew he was swearing. He knew he was using language that would cause his sisters to ground him, but he didn't care. Trying to take Jasper's weight wasn't solving the problem. Jasper was fighting him to break free. At least that was promising. "Don't you dare, you bastard! You do not get to do this!"

Charlie let him go. He grabbed the chair, leapt onto it, and hacked straight through the rope with his clay knife. Jasper hit the ground hard. He gave a sharp yelp, but Charlie barely heard it over the sound of blood ringing in his ears. He grabbed the noose from the back, pulling it up, slipping the blade under, and ripping through it so that Jasper couldn't try and choke himself with it on the floor.

Jasper was still fighting him, but it was fast becoming pointless. He glanced up and the fight went out of him instantly. Charlie didn't know what he looked like, shirtless and spattered with clay, a big knife in one hand and the hacked up rope in the other, but he didn't think he'd ever been so angry in his life. Not anger like this. Pure, absolute rage, utterly untinged by other emotions.

He was panting, gasping like he'd run a race. He wasn't sure if it was from the panic or the exertion.

Jasper took one look at him, and curled into a defeated ball of shame and misery on the ground. Charlie ran out of energy. He leant against the wall and slowly sank down to the floor, facing Jasper.

"You absolute cock," Charlie cursed him, his voice thick with exhaustion and disgust. "What gives you the right?!"

Jasper began to laugh. He sprawled on the floor opposite Charlie and he laughed softly like a man who had lost all semblance of sanity. Charlie muttered more violent curses under his breath, shaking his head.

"She made me tell her, you know," Jasper wheezed on the floor. "She knew already, of course, but she came here and she made me tell her. She gave me this." He pointed to his nose. It was mostly too dark to see, but Charlie could make out a small amount of bruising.

"What?" he muttered, uncomfortably aware that Jasper was probably mad.

"Your doctor, Charlie," Jasper laughed and wept at the same time. He pulled himself slowly off the floor until he was sitting opposite Charlie. "Your Doctor Florin. She came by… and she asked me about Susan and Rebecca's wedding…"

Charlie felt his blood ice over. The hallway was suddenly freezing and goosebumps prickled his bare skin.

"How…?" he breathed. "How?! How, Jasper? What— what did you tell her?"

"Everything," Jasper shrugged. "She already knew though."

"How did she know?!" Charlie demanded.

Jasper turned to regard him in the darkness, and he looked strangely sane given what they were going through.

"You really didn't tell her…" he whispered.

"No!" Charlie gasped. "She… she doesn't know…"

"Huh," Jasper looked away. "She does know, Charlie. She knows everything. I assumed you told her, even though she said you didn't. She said Julian said something."

"Julian doesn't know," Charlie insisted. "No one knows."

"Then maybe your doctor really is as good as you are after all," Jasper mused. "She's got us pegged, certainly."

Charlie sat in that and stewed. He didn't know how long they sat like that. He was strangely dizzy and it warped the passage of time. He was cold and getting colder. Everything felt strangely dream-like and unreal. Eventually, Jasper coughed.

"You should have let me hang, Charlie," he muttered. "I'm not going to prison. I'd rather die."

"You're not going to prison," Charlie told him disgustedly. "Prison doesn't help anyone. It's not going to help us." He looked over at Jasper and their eyes met. The hopelessness in Jasper's eyes did nothing to temper his anger, which was still bitterly fresh and raw. "But you don't get to do this. You keep making messes for other people to clean up and making it out to be my fault. You're not doing this. Not this time. It stops now."

Charlie staggered up from the floor. He left the knife and the rope on the chair and then hauled Jasper to his feet, ignoring his protests. The butler was injured, but not badly. He had some notable scrapes and bruises but, as far as Charlie was concerned, he deserved those. Jasper may have been making a point of resisting, but he didn't resist hard enough to affect the outcome. Charlie couldn't help but think that was quite typically them.

He dragged Jasper, struggling and protesting, straight into his sisters' room. He didn't knock. Fortunately, he seemed to be interrupting their sleep rather than anything he may have wished to avoid.

"Charlie?" Rebecca startled sleepily, sitting up as he came in and turned on their light. "Jasper?"

"What's going on?" Susan added, also sitting up and pulling the blankets around her nightdress.

Charlie hauled Jasper into the room so that he couldn't get away. In proper light, the bruising around his nose was more visible, and so were the fresh marks around his throat. He had stopped struggling now that he was faced with Susan and Rebecca. He stood with his face downcast like a pillar of shame.

"Jasper has something to tell you," Charlie announced. "And once he's told you, then the three of you can work out what to do next. Whether he goes to a clinic, seeks new employment, or stays here, I truly don't care, but psychotherapy is non-negotiable. He needs help."

"Charlie—!" Rebecca began.

"I'm done," Charlie told them, also staring at the floor as he said it, still gripping Jasper's wrist like he wasn't really sure if he was ever going to let go.

Both women stared at them in shock, unsure what to make of such an interruption. Neither man would meet their eyes. Charlie turned, not wanting to stick around for what was going to happen. He risked a glance at Jasper. Jasper met his look.

"Tell them everything," Charlie ordered. "All of it. They will make sure you get the help you need. Regular therapy, Jasper. But I'm done. This is all the help you get from me."

He left them at that, shutting the door behind him on the way out and leaving the anger in the room behind him. He was utterly empty without it. He trudged down the stairs to his room, but there was no peace there. His room was just another room of this Godforsaken house Rebecca had dragged him to. The whole house was just memories of him and Jasper, and Jasper's endless reminders. Charlie couldn't stay in it. He couldn't sit and stew. He pulled on some proper clothes, donned his pale coat, and strode out into the night.

There were still faint lights on in the depths of the bakery across the road. Charlie stood on the front steps of his house and stared at them for a long time. Michael and Julian were in there. Those two had been so happy to see each other again. Charlie remembered the genuine love in their expressions when they saw each other. He didn't want to disturb them. Not now.

He turned and walked off up the street, letting his feet lead him through the city he knew so well. In so many ways, the city was more of a home to him than any one building. Though he did remember the simple days of Bronny's High House very fondly. He remembered his family home with a love for a place unlike anything he'd known elsewhere. Even the old church. His father's church. That was a place he remembered… not fondly. He had fond memories of it. But they had held his father's funeral there. It was all he thought of when he saw the place. He wouldn't go back to it anymore. Church, Charlie knew well, was not really a place for someone like him.

His feet walked him to Hyde Park as though in a dream. The circus was long gone, and it was nice to be able to sit on a bench in the dark, watching the small light of the lanterns illuminate the walkways like trails of stars. He felt like he shouldn't be alone. This time of night there was always someone about, even post the Jack of Hearts. It was amazing how quickly a city could recover from terror. Memories were short. Especially collective ones.

Charlie wished his memory was short. He wished one of the old wanderers he used to trade cough syrup with was around. That might even dull the ache, or at least alleviate the dizziness that was still plaguing him. He looked around, searching for signs of anyone else. There really wasn't anyone. He was completely alone.

That was nice. It was nice to finally just be on his own.

Charlie buried his face in his arms and began to weep. It went from zero to a hundred faster than a speeding train. There had been nothing, and now there was only pain. He cried so hard he couldn't breathe. His head hurt. It was pounding. The sobs came from everywhere, not just deep in his lungs, but from all the way in his toes. It felt like being thrown down a waterfall. He cried so hard he thought he might suffocate and die right there on the park bench.

After everything else, wouldn't that have been a way to go?

The only reason he was here was because he had no idea where to go.

But that was a lie. He knew exactly where to go. He just didn't know how to make himself go there. The answer was simple. One foot in front of the other. It didn't calm him. It didn't save him from himself, but it wasn't asking much, and after everything he'd done for everyone else, it was the least he could do for himself.

Amy woke to the sounds of supressed sobbing. She hadn't heard the window open and close. He must have done that very silently. Of course, her room was two floors above ground and she didn't expect anyone to climb to it. She should have panicked, but she knew what was happening as soon as she heard it, and someone breaking into her room was, perhaps foolishly, the least of her concerns.

"Charlie!" she exclaimed, throwing back the covers and leaping from the bed. She straightened her nightdress as she hurried over to him. He was curled up under her windowsill, beside her dresser. He had his knees up by his face, weeping into them. She collapsed down beside him and threw her arms around him. "Charlie! Darling, you're freezing!"

He was hyperventilating worse than he had on the floor at the inn. She held him close, rubbing his back and taking loud slow breaths to try and encourage him to mimic the behaviour.

"I'm sorry—" he gasped. "I—I didn't know where—where else—to go—"

"It's okay," she whispered, kissing his hair. "It's okay, Charlie. You're okay." He was like ice in her hands, and both of them sitting on the floor together was only making her cold. "Okay, shoes and coat, Charlie." She coaxed him out of both. He didn't fight her. He was still crying, his breath was still trembling, but he let her help him out of his muddy shoes and battered coat.

She left him fully dressed as she dragged him into the bed with her and tucked the blankets tightly around them both, holding him gently. She tried to take her mother's advice. Charlie needed space, but he also just needed a hug from a friend who didn't want anything from him. Amy knew she could do that right now. All she wanted was for her Charlie to be all right. So, she held him gently in the blankets while he cried. Slowly, they both warmed up. She stroked his hair and kissed his forehead and just let his sorrow run its course. Finally, once his tears had eased and his breathing had steadied, he spoke, and his words sent a horrified chill through her blood.

"Jasper tried to hang himself tonight," he whispered.

"Oh God..." Amy breathed.

"I stopped him," Charlie continued. "He's okay. I left him with Rebecca and Susan. They'll get him help. He'll… he'll be okay."

"Charlie, I'm so sorry—" Amy began, guilt flooding her like burst dam.

"It's not your fault," he assured. "Truly, Amy. We are not responsible for his actions. Not this time. He got there all on his own."

"Charlie… I…" Amy began, choking on the guilt as she tried to whisper the truth.

"Hit him in the face today?" Charlie murmured. He nuzzled in against her, his cold nose pressed to her cheek, but his breath warm on her skin. "I saw that." He paused again and Amy couldn't bring herself to elaborate, but she didn't have to. Charlie continued. "He said you knew. He said you knew about it. About us."

"I suspected," she whispered. "Michael and Julian suspected. I got the hints from them. After… well, after…"

"After what happened at the inn…" Charlie muttered.

"I didn't mean to trigger you," Amy apologised.

"I didn't mean to get triggered," he replied. She wanted to tell him no one ever meant to get triggered and it was a silly thing to say, but his body tensed for a moment, his arms tightening around her as he shifted slightly, and then he continued. "It's strange… I never think about it. Barely even remember it. I was drunk, you know. It was the first time I'd ever been drunk. Proper blackout. I don't really remember. I thought I didn't…"

"But you did…" she whispered.

"But I did," he agreed. "When… when you were on top of me in the bed… suddenly… suddenly I was back in Jasper's bed, under him—" Charlie stopped abruptly. She didn't blame him. She wasn't really sure she wanted to hear, but she was prepared to listen if he needed to say it. Nothing more seemed forthcoming.

"It's not your fault, Charlie," she told him.

He laughed bitterly.

"It's not!" she insisted.

"It's not *not* my fault," he replied.

"You were just a boy!" she protested. "You were taken advantage of!"

"I wasn't just a boy, Amy," he whispered. "I know I was young, but… but I knew what I was doing. I knew what I was doing right up until I didn't, and then it was too late for either of us. Besides… I— I must— part of me must have— I couldn't have otherwise…"

"Charlie," Amy shut him down firmly. "While it is admirable that you feel you ought to take responsibility for your part in what happened, you were fourteen, and you didn't want it — and before you start up about what physically occurred again, I would just like to say that while I might not have any personal experience with fourteen year old boys, I have a medical and physiological understanding, and that understanding tells me that most boys that age can be aroused by a brick."

Charlie laughed softly into her shoulder. She could feel him tremble in her arms again, and she wasn't sure if he was just laughing or laughing and crying. Either way, she stroked his hair comfortingly while she waited for it to pass.

"You want it not to be my fault," he whispered.

"It wasn't—" she insisted.

"That attitude is why I never told anyone," he admitted.

Amy froze. She shifted back from him, just a little. She needed to meet his eye. She needed to know she'd heard that correctly. He blinked at her tragically in the dark, his grey eyes like misty dawn on a dreary day.

"Charlie…" she began, but she had heard him right, and now she was speechless.

"Society likes crime to be simple," he told her softly. "Look at everything we've been through. Everyone wants it to be easy. A bad thing happens, there is an obvious perpetrator and an obvious victim, and justice is served by arresting the perpetrator and throwing them in prison." Charlie blinked softly in the darkness. His eyes were imploring as he searched her face. "Life isn't that simple, Amy, and prison doesn't help. This was a crime of two victims and the system isn't built to handle that. If we'd been sober… it never would have happened. If we'd been sober… Jasper might have kissed me, but I would have stopped it there. This wasn't an assault, Amy. It wasn't like Jasper snuck into my room and preyed on me. That's what everyone wants it to be, but it wasn't. I was in his bed, getting drunk with him in his bedroom, with wine I had stolen from my sister's wedding party. I was rebelling against her. I was fighting Becky for marrying a noblewoman. I did know, Amy. I just… I didn't think it was real. I didn't think anyone would actually want me like that… and then we were too drunk to communicate and it was too late. I was too drunk to stop him and he was too drunk to know I wanted to stop."

Amy took a deep breath. "That doesn't mean he gets a free pass, Charlie. What he did to you—"

"Was wrong," Charlie nodded. "I understand what you're saying, I do, but I know I was partly at fault — and I knew if I ever tried to tell anyone what happened no one would listen to that part, because of my age, because of my sister, because of the class system. No one was going to let me own it. They would only persecute Jasper, and I don't think he deserves that."

"That's awfully big of you, Charlie," Amy replied, trying to keep the judgement from her voice. She wasn't sure she succeeded.

"Amy," he started again patiently. "If I had gotten drunk that night and climbed a tree and fallen out and broken my arm, everyone would have been content with the narrative that I had made a drunken mistake, hurt myself, and learnt a valuable lesson. Well, I fell out of the tree and broke my arm and learnt that lesson. It's just that Jasper fell out of the tree too and he might have broken a lot more than just his arm."

"All right," Amy conceded. "But, Charlie, I don't know if this is you trying to take control and own your situation, or if this is what you truly believe, but I think you're overlooking the part where Jasper pushed you up that tree."

"I showed Jasper where the tree was," Charlie

countered. "Amy, I'm not trying to negate Jasper's guilt — Jasper is still very guilty and he did wrong, but he's not a bad person and he doesn't deserve to be vilified for the mistake — which wouldn't help anyone and would only make things worse."

"Hm," Amy supplied. She wanted to be supportive. She wanted so badly to support Charlie through this, but he had yet to convince her that Jasper wasn't, in fact, a bad person. Charlie seemed to know she was struggling.

"You know I believe in rehabilitation not punishment," Charlie reminded. "Jasper needs help, not condemning. He learnt his lesson too. It's not like anything like this ever happened again. It's not like my silence put others in danger. The Quids have served the Guineas for generations, and while I personally have strong moral objections to servitude, Jasper loves Susan and would do anything for her. I broke his heart — I never meant to, but I did — and then he was forced to wait on me every day or find a new job. I'm not surprised he became as bitter as he did, especially when even mentioning the truth would risk his arrest. He didn't know."

"He didn't take the time to know," Amy retorted, unable to help herself. "You didn't find a drunk man and pounce on him, Charlie. Jasper made assumptions about you and then didn't check and those assumptions proved woefully incorrect. Also, his behaviour in response to the incident has been appalling."

"Amy, please —"

"Appalling, Charlie," she insisted. "However, you

need not plead. If I was going to betray him, I would have done it by now. Your secret is safe with me." She brushed her curled fingers against his cheek. "I love you, Charlie. All I want is for you to be okay. I will support whatever you need, as long as I don't think you're doing more harm."

He curled into her, resting his face in the crook of her neck and holding her close.
"Thank you," he whispered against her skin. His breath tickled, but she also curled into it. His slight frame fit surprisingly well curled against the curves of her body. They stayed cuddled together, supporting each other, until sleep eventually took them.

15

Early morning was accompanied by a distant and frantic knocking. At first, Charlie wondered what was ailing Rebecca, then he realised he had woken next to Amy, in her bed, and that there was no reason for Rebecca to be there. Amy also woke to the noise and the two immediately shared a look of unified panic at the thought of trying to explain what had happened.

Charlie leapt from the bed and quickly donned his shoes and jacket. He was vaguely aware that the scruffy state of yesterday's clothes was not going to do him any favours in this situation. Amy joined him in bounding from the bed and hurriedly pulled on her dressing gown and slippers.

Voices were drifting up from downstairs. Charlie could hear Rebecca. By the time he was on the stairs, he could hear Henry. That certainly gave him a pause of concern... and fear. Mostly fear. But there was no helping it, and he didn't want to try being dishonest. Not about spending the night in Amy's bed.

"Please, Lord Pound," Rebecca's urgent tone carried up to them as they crept surreptitiously down the stairs. "He's missing. I don't know where he's gone. He's not at home, he's not at the bakery... something's happened, Henry, something big, and… and I just —"

"Take a breath, my Lady," Henry advised. "I haven't seen him. Digby and Penny say the staff haven't seen him either. But it's Shilling, he will show up. I can have someone check the local jails in case he went soapboxing again."

Rebecca said nothing. Rebecca said nothing because she was standing with Henry Pound, Digby, and Penny in the entrance hall and she could see Charlie and Amy descending the stairs like a bad pantomime. Pound and his staff seemed to realise something was happening behind them and turned. Charlie stopped as he reached the bottom of the stairs, aware of Amy halted just behind him. He was certain that it looked worse than it was.

Pound's expression was immediately and violently loud, but it paused just as quickly. So did the judgement of everyone else. Charlie could see Amy's reflection in the polished balustrade, frantically shaking her head and gesturing at them all. Charlie almost smiled.

"It's not what it looks like," he told Henry. He had no idea how he'd earnt enough goodwill with Pound for such credence, or if his Lordship was just taking his daughter's urgent signing at face value, but Henry gave him a slight nod and the outrage went out of his expression.

"All right, Mister Shilling," he accepted gruffly.

The next thing that happened was Rebecca colliding with him at speed. She threw her arms around his neck and squeezed him like he'd been missing for weeks. It knocked the air out of his lungs.

"Charlie!" she gasped, clutching at him like she was trying to crack a rib.

"I'm sorry I scared you," he wheezed.

She stopped squeezing him long enough to take his face in her hands, forcing him to meet her eye. Her eyes were full of unshed tears and Charlie wished he didn't have to look at them.

"Oh Charlie…" she murmured, choking up.

"Why don't the two of you step into the parlour and I'll have Penny bring you some tea," Amy suggested, ushering them out of the public eye.

"We don't need—" Charlie began.

"You love tea, Charlie, and it's good for you," Amy told him. "I'll help her make it, if that will ease your socialist conscience."

It did not particularly help, but he didn't have time to say that before Amy shut him in the parlour with his sister. It was still early and the room was cold with residual night. He was glad he had his coat, as the sudden absence of blankets over his clothes was chilling. Charlie and Rebecca stood by the door, neither moving. For a moment, Charlie just cocked his head and listened. Rebecca let him.

"Amelia, what on Earth—?" Pound began in a hushed tone on the other side of the door.

"Please be gentle with him, Daddy," Amy implored softly. "He's having a breakdown."

"Is it to do with—" and that time Pound cut himself off. They were, after all, not alone.

"It's probably to do with a lot of things," Amy sighed. "Starting long before we had anything to do with him. Just… please, Daddy— Penny! Stop eavesdropping and come help me make tea!"

"Oh, that's not necessary, Doctor—" Penny's voice joined the discussion.

"It is, trust me," Amy sighed. "He'll know."

"I know he's an odd duck, Doctor Florin, but he's let me make tea for him before—" Penny insisted, footsteps echoing over her voice as it grew distant.

"I know, Penny, but he's very fragile this morning," Amy replied. More soft footfalls joined the clipping of Penny's heels and Charlie could hear everyone moving away from the door now. That meant there was nothing to listen to. Nothing out there, anyway.

Rebecca was still looking at him. It was the same way she'd looked at him when their father had died and he did not like it. There was heartbreak in her eyes. He did not want that to be his fault. He stood with his head tilted, stimming his ring, and watching it twist at a comforting and consistent speed around his finger.

"Charlie…" Rebecca murmured, taking him by the shoulders. "Are you all right?"

He nodded.

"Are you really?" she checked.

He nodded again.

"Charlie, look at me, please," she requested.

Charlie twisted his head this way and that, trying to comply but unable to. He couldn't make himself look up at her. He wished she hadn't asked.

"Charlie, why did you never tell me?" she pressed.

He shook his head. He couldn't raise his eyes to meet hers and she was asking hard questions. He just wanted to be left alone. It was over again. Jasper was getting help. He could go back to ignoring it. He'd told Amy. He'd be okay now.

"Sweetheart," Rebecca continued softly, "I know you like things to be logical, and you don't like big displays of emotion, but I need to know how you're feeling right now, okay? I need you to express those feelings — even just verbally list it for me."

"I do emote," Charlie muttered, staring at his shoes and spinning his ring and hiding behind his hair. "I do, Becky. I'm doing it. Amy knows. Amy can see it."

"Do you want me to get her in here with us?" Rebecca asked.

Charlie shook his head. That would make it worse. Amy might be good at translating him, but he did not want her to see him like this. Not again. They'd just done this.

"She helps, doesn't she?" Becky said. "You love her very much, don't you, Charlie?"

He closed his eyes and nodded slowly, easing the speed with which he fidgeted. The smooth metal slowed in his fingers and he felt himself calming. The dark helped. Amy helped.

"She's a safe space for you. Is that why you could tell her?" Rebecca continued.

"I didn't tell her," Charlie whispered. "I didn't tell her anything. She worked it out. The whole thing, even down to Jasper. She solved it. Becky… why did you make us share a room? Why did you do that?"

"Because I didn't know," she told him. "I'm sorry, Charlie. I'm so sorry. If I'd known, if I'd had any idea, I never would have done it. I thought it was a cheeky little joke, a little encouragement because I knew you two liked each other. I had no idea what I was pushing you into."

Charlie nodded, but he didn't open his eyes. That made sense. He didn't begrudge her. He could see how that was the kind of joke she would play. It was the kind of joke any of their friends would play. Julian, Michael, Laura, and Jane… all of them would have done that to each other and thought it was funny. If someone had done that to Julian and Michael back when Charlie was trying to matchmake them, he would have thought it was funny. He could understand why setting him and Amy up like that was funny. Why wasn't he laughing?

"I didn't tell her…" he whispered.

Becky rubbed his arms reassuringly and rested her forehead against his.

"I know, Charlie," she whispered. "I believe you. She's very clever."

"No, I… I didn't tell her…" he whispered, dropping his voice even softer. "I had every opportunity, and I didn't tell her that I love her."

Becky gave a small breath of laughter and Charlie felt it warm his cheeks.

"I think she knows, darling." Rebecca paused, holding him gently but firmly and keeping her face pressed to his.

He liked when they did this. She used to do it when he got overstimulated as a boy. They would sit with their eyes closed and foreheads together and she would tell him to focus on her and ignore the world. List the things he could sense about her. It had been years since he'd used Rebecca as a coping mechanism. He was supposed to be old enough to cope alone now. But she was holding him like he was still her little brother. He supposed he was.

"Charlie…" she whispered, keeping her tone in line with him. "Please, darling, why didn't you tell me about Jasper?"

"Because…" he murmured.

"Because what, Charlie?" she pressed.

"Because it was your wedding, Becky," he answered.

The truth of it was sobering. There were lots of reasons he hadn't said anything. He hadn't wanted to punish Jasper. He hadn't wanted to make anything of it. He'd just wanted to recover from his hangover and forget. And he had. Mostly. It had been a long time until he'd realised that hadn't really worked. By then it was too late to act on. It was well past. Best left ignored. But the big truth, the one he knew was at the core of his silence to the one person he truly should have told, was that one. It was her wedding. She deserved that day. He had never meant to tarnish it.

Rebecca seemed to understand that. Charlie could feel her comprehension from the single line in the way she pulled him into her arms, buried her face in his shoulder, and started to cry. He had not meant to make her cry. He was worried he was also going to start now. He did not like to see her unhappy. He hadn't meant to cause this. Slowly, his arms crept up her back, embracing her in return, and squeezing tightly.

"I'm sorry, Becky," he muttered.

"I'm sorry, Charlie," she wept. "I'm so sorry, darling. I can't believe I never noticed. I just thought you two had some kind of… I don't even know. All these years, I thought you were just riling each other up. I… I guess… I guess I thought if it was something serious, you'd tell me. I didn't know you were keeping such big secrets. I wish I'd known, Charlie."

"I'm sorry," he muttered. "I… I can't change it…"

"It's okay." She pulled his head in tightly and kissed his cheek. He could feel her tears on his skin. "It's okay, sweetheart. I just… I'm your sister, Charles. You need to tell me the big things. I can't fix them if you don't."

"You can't fix the big things, Becky," he smiled. "No one person can."

"I'm not talking about helping you overthrow the monarchy, Charlie," she sighed. "I'm talking about making sure your home is safe for you to live in."

"Home is safe for me to live in," he replied.

"Really?" she pressed.

"Yes," he assured. "I've never been in danger from Jasper, Becky. Not real danger."

"Well, we're dealing to it," she promised.

"What are you doing?" he asked. "What's happening?"

"We haven't decided yet," she replied. "We wanted to talk to you."

"I don't care," he told her, slowly but firmly untangling himself from her embrace. "I told you when I left that I didn't care."

"You really don't care?" she demanded, blinking down at him, her face blotchy and tearstained.

"I really don't," he confirmed. Then he realised what he was saying and paused. Expressions chased each other quickly across his face. "I don't want you to fire Jasper," he added.

Rebecca delicately wiped at her eyes and waited. She knew there was more. They had done this dance many times. Charlie was processing and she was going to let him take his time to list his demands. He had a feeling she might accept more of them than usual in this instance, but possibly not too.

"I don't want you to fire Jasper," he repeated. "But if he wants to leave on his own terms, then I think we should help him find employment or care elsewhere, especially if he thinks he needs to go into a clinic for a while to recover. I don't want him to go to prison. You can't have him arrested."

"Can't we?" Rebecca raised a cool eyebrow, trying to look confident despite her snuffles.

"No, Becky, you can't," Charlie insisted. "Prison never does any good. Who do you think it would help? Certainly not Jasper. Rebecca, it's impossible to stop bad things from happening. I've looked into it. There will always be disasters, and there will always be humans making mistakes. All we can do is help those who realise their errors, and educate those who don't." Charlie sighed deeply.

Rebecca knew how he felt about this, and he realised as he looked at her that she was baiting him a little. She knew that vocalising his beliefs would help. It did. Charlie could feel himself beginning to stitch back together like a darned pocket as he argued with her.

"Becky," he continued, soothed by his conviction. "Jasper knows he was in the wrong. His years of petty behaviour hide a pain deeper than mine. He never meant to hurt me, and I never meant to hurt him. But mistakes were made, on both sides, and we have both already been punished enough. He only did what he did last night because he knows he was wrong. He's known this whole time. It's… it's why he acts out…" Charlie realised he'd never quite put those pieces together before. He'd known why, but he hadn't known *why*. "Becky, Jasper blamed me and took it out on me, because he needed it to be my fault. In his head, if it wasn't my fault, then he had done something utterly unforgiveable and he wouldn't be able to live with that. I… I didn't realise it was so bad for him. I was too busy trying to ignore it for myself, but I swore him to secrecy, which kept either of us from getting help. Jasper had to look at his mistake and wait on it every day. That is punishment. I already punished him, and I didn't mean to. Becky, please, you cannot have him arrested."

"I won't," she agreed stoically.

"And I don't want you to fire him either," Charlie insisted.

She breathed out loudly through her nose.

"I mean it," Charlie said. "I know it will be harder for you to have him around than me, but if he wants to stay, as long as he's getting help, I don't mind. He's known Susan all his life. I don't want to force him away."

"You're very forgiving, Charlie," Rebecca murmured.

"What's the point in being anything else?" he shrugged.

Rebecca gave him a long and considered look. She had a tinge of frustration about her, as though she was stuck arguing with a monk. Then she pulled him back into her arms. He didn't fight it and stayed content in her embrace for as long as she needed. There were worse places to be, and at least he didn't have to meet anyone's eye. Rebecca heaved a deep sigh.

"When Amy brings that tea through, are we going to stage an intervention so that you can tell her you love her?" she asked.

"No," Charlie replied, having no desire to be involved in such a ploy and feeling that the time and the moment were certainly not right. "Actually, Becky, after tea… I would like to… to just go home."

She squeezed him again. He was starting to feel like a stress sponge. It really wasn't so bad.

"All right, darling," she agreed. "That sounds good."

The strangest thing about the next couple of weeks was that everyone insisted Jasper wasn't the only one to get help. Charlie felt like everyone he knew was insisting he also attend therapy. It seemed wholly unnecessary, until Amy pointed out that she'd helped him through at least two panic attacks, and that if he met anyone else who was going through even half of what he'd survived, he would insist they get help too. She was annoyingly good at making perfect sense.

He was annoyingly good at being immovably stubborn.

They were forced to reach a compromise. Charlie agreed to talk, but only to Michael Pence. His Skipper was the only person Charlie trusted with enough insight into his character to help him, who wasn't also tangled in his issues. Michael was safe, and everyone else agreed that was a start. Michael also knew. He already knew everything — far more than Charlie had ever given him credit for. It was almost like he'd been waiting for Charlie to need to talk about it, and now he was here and he was ready. Not to mention, he was extraordinarily patient for a man planning his wedding.

A wedding to Julian Silver, no less.

But it was a lovely wedding. Small, intimate, lowkey. The Sovereigns attended basically in disguise. Julian used his legally changed name — another loophole by which he had found to shove it to his late father. He also managed to get through vows and speeches without saying anything anyone would regret. Amy and Charlie had been helping him with that. They were confident he was trying to be on his best behaviour for Michael.

Skipp's face was healing nicely, and the grooms made a handsome couple, or so Charlie logically and completely unbiasedly thought. He sat at the back of the reception as the night wore on, content in the half-light as he watched his loved ones enjoy themselves. They deserved this. It was nice, on occasion, to get to watch good things happen to good people.

He was not surprised in the slightest when company

joined him on the stools at the back. There was a part of him that was even pleased. Amy slipped carefully onto the stool at his side, lounging beside him. She was in red tonight. She always looked good in red. He was trying not to look. There was nothing left to notice that he hadn't noticed immediately upon seeing her before the ceremony. Nothing but her expression, and he wasn't sure he trusted himself to look at that.

"How are you doing, Charlie?" she asked softly, her voice accompanied by music the band in the corner played, and nearly drowned out by the cheering and laughter coming from the other end of the room.

"Fine," he nodded, trying to convey his contentment with more outward expression. Rebecca had been attempting to coax more out of him recently. He realised as he was doing it that Amy could read him just fine without it, and it probably looked like bizarre behaviour to her. He settled again.

"You're not drinking tonight?" she commented. She was trying to be subtle about it, but he knew when he was being checked on.

"Never at weddings," he answered. It didn't require elaboration, and they both knew that, but he was worried about the uncomfortable tone that left them sitting in, so he tried. "I only drink on special occasions."

"Like funerals and between cases?" Amy laughed. She smiled at him like she understood, but it was still warning. "Don't let the grooms catch you saying that."

Charlie pulled a face. "Never weddings," he insisted, before allowing himself a thoughtful pause. "I will concede, however, that this one is rather special..." He smiled. "Skipp did tell me he would find me a wedding I wouldn't protest attending one day. I should have realised he meant his own."

"I'm glad you didn't protest," she smiled, bumping his shoulder affectionately with hers. "I would have felt awfully out of place up there without you."

"Nonsense," Charlie shook his head. "You risked your life to protect his little brother, Florin — that makes you family."

"Between us," she whispered close to his ear as they watched the festivities, "I'd just as soon not be part of their family. I've had more than enough drama with just my own."

He would concede her that. For the logic of it more than the warmth of her breath on his cheek, but that didn't hurt either.

"Have you heard from your mother again?" he asked.

"She wrote to me," Amy nodded. "She said she'd let me know next time she was in London."

Charlie nodded. That was good. It was nice that she was able to have things start to come right for her. She deserved that.

Why didn't he feel like everything was working out? It was. Everyone was happy. Things were right in the world again, even if some wrongs had been committed to get there. All right, he hadn't dismantled the oppressive class system that was throttling society or overthrown capitalism yet, but things were still okay. His friends were well and happy.

"Charlie…" Amy murmured, leaning in against him again. "Can I get you anything? I know you don't want to drink, but you look like you need… well… something—"

"Thank you, Florin, but I'm all right," he replied. "I think we both know, given the option, I'd usually go for something stronger than wine or ale anyway, if I could get it." He didn't look at her when he said it. He didn't want to see how she was looking at him, just in case it wasn't good. He didn't have a problem, but he knew how people could be about such things. He knew how doctors could be about the overuse of medicines when one wasn't technically unwell. Still, he wanted to argue that when he medicated it was because he wasn't well, except he didn't know how to explain it to someone who had never experienced it.

"That's because you're severely sensitive to overstimulation," Amy told him.

Now, Charlie turned to look at her. Her green eyes were dark in the shadows they loitered in, but she watched him with such understanding and patience, like she was reading his mind. She slipped a hand into his, linking their fingers and pulling his hand back towards her so that she could clasp it in both of hers.

"When you're working, you can focus on your work and block out the distractions, but other times you're vulnerable to the bright, loud stress of the world, and you need other things to dull your senses for you," she stated, tracing the back of his hand soothingly with her thumb and watching the pattern she made. Her eyes flicked up to meet his with a gentle smile. "It's not as uncommon as people make you think it is, Charlie."

Charlie stared at her like she was the most incredible person in the world. Because she was.

"Flo— uh, Amy…" he stammered. She looked at him expectantly. He looked around. They were alone, but there were still celebrations going on in the room, and it was abruptly loud. Not that the volume had changed, just that he had. He slipped off his stool, but he didn't let go of her hand.

She took the hint, following him down and around the corner, under the bound drapes that hung over the alcove, and deeper into the shadows. He held her hand tighter as he led her away, but didn't take her far. He didn't want to drag her from the party.

"God, I hope there's not a secret passage down here," she muttered, as they slunk away from the noise. "I'm not ready for another case. We only just finished the Sovereign one."

"That wasn't a real case," Charlie muttered back. "We didn't solve a mystery, we barely resolved a domestic dispute."

Florin snorted and he stopped, turning to face her. He could still see everyone out in the well-lit end of the hall, talking and dancing, but at least the little nook felt almost private, and he needed some shelter to say this.

"Amy, I need to say something, and I've been meaning to say it for some time," he told her, feeling a strange panic clutch his chest.

"I know, Charlie," she smiled softly.

"No," he shook his head. "That's not fair. You told me that you love me, more than once now, and I never said it back. I'm confident that I had a host of reasons for that, but I am certain that none of them were good, because I do love you, Amy. I have for a long time now. You are the smartest, kindest, most wonderful person I have ever met, and I'm sorry I didn't say this sooner. I've known that I loved you since France, which can only mean I was afflicted earlier —"

"Afflicted?" she echoed.

Charlie winced. "That was not perhaps— Can I go back—?"

"To before you said 'afflicted'?" she checked. He winced again. Then her laughter breathed in his ear and he was pulled into her affectionate embrace. She kissed his cheek. "I know you far too well, Charlie, to be offended by that."

He closed his eyes in relief and tightened his arms protectively around her, like they could exist for a moment in their own little bubble. She always understood. Better than anyone ever had before. Better than he'd ever believed anyone could.

"I do love you, Amy," he whispered, holding her close. "In a completely different way to anyone before. These feelings are… they're new to me."

She released him, but they didn't quite let each other go; only moving back enough to meet each other's eyes. He could meet her eyes. They weren't intimidating or confusing. He could meet her gaze, even hold it. It was like looking into the eyes of Athena, pure wisdom behind a midnight scattering of black freckles. Her hands tightened on his sleeves as they gazed at each other.

"Really since France?" she asked, genuine surprise in her voice.

"Really," he nodded. "I'm sorry I didn't say sooner."

"So am I," she admitted. "But I think perhaps we were right not to. So much has happened…"

"We might have messed it up earlier," he finished.

"Quite," she agreed.

"We might still mess it up now," he added, unable to stop himself.

"We might," she agreed.

"I would really like to kiss you now…" he murmured.

"In public?" She shot a look out to the party just beyond the fastened drapes.

Charlie dropped his eyes apologetically. Inappropriate. Obviously inappropriate.

"Of course, sorry," he muttered.

But her hand was on his cheek and she was moving closer. And it was Amelia Florin, of course she didn't think it was inappropriate. Of course she was teasing him. It was one of the many ways she kept him tactfully on edge. He appreciated that. He also appreciated the way her face fitted perfectly in his hands, and the soft warmth of her lips as her mouth opened against his. The soft floral scent of her that had been easing his nerves for months now. Mostly. She really was rather perfect.

He kissed her like it was the first time all over again. Somehow, their entire relationship had been built on a matchstick tower of first times. This was a new first. It tasted like lipstick and roses. It tasted like the death of all the maybes and almosts they had carefully skirted since they began. It tasted like the life of something new. Something certain. Because he was certain. This time, he was certain, and he'd never been more certain of anything. He loved her. And he wanted her. And he was kissing her. In public. There was an entire room of people who could see them. He wasn't scared. Not this time.

His hands were in her hair and he was trying not to muss her curls, but he couldn't let her go, not even if he'd wanted to. When his mouth left hers, he was gasping like she'd drawn the breath from his lungs. But she was no better. Her eyes were closed and she rested her forehead against his, her hands on his cheeks and her lips loitering by his as though they feared to stray too far.

"I love you too, Charlie," she whispered. "I want this... whatever it is... and I'm happy to move at whatever speed you need to move at."

Charlie gave a small nod, that mostly seemed to manifest as brushing his face against hers.

"I... I was thinking... thinking that I would drop you home after the wedding," he suggested.

"That would be lovely," she replied, not moving back from him or stating that he would have done that no matter what occurred tonight.

"Perhaps..." he whispered. "Perhaps, depending on your condition and inclination, I... I could stay... if you wanted...?"

The question hung there and he wished he hadn't suggested it. That was almost certainly too far. It was just that she made him bold, and in matters such as these she was far more confident than he was. He'd thought she might have appreciated the offer. Still, she had made no move to let him go. Given the way things were turning out, it was probably about time he stopped making assumptions about Amelia Florin. She wasn't like anyone else he knew. For a start, she kept proving him wrong. Her fingers slipped around the back of his neck, somehow pulling him closer.

"What do you think?" he asked.

"I think…" she whispered onto his lips, "that I'm going to make Julian and his friends drink the rest of those bottles on their own." Her mouth brushed against his in a way that somehow wasn't a kiss, but teased him that it could be. "Because I'd really like you to take me home later."

There wasn't space to say anything more, so he kissed her again. Her grip around his neck tightened as she seemed to melt against him, dripping over him. Another hour or two at the wedding suddenly seemed like a lifetime. Still, they'd waited this long already. He was confident they could manage. He was in love with Amelia Florin, and she had made it unequivocally clear she loved him back. He was confident he could manage anything.

Thus concludes *The Case of Silver & Sovereign* Book Four of the *Shilling & Florin Mysteries*. The story continues in
BOOK FIVE:
A COLD & BITTER REVENGE

Did you enjoy this book?

Please consider leaving a review for it on Amazon or Goodreads. Every positive review allows me to spend more time writing books for you to enjoy!

katehaleyauthor/amazon

OTHER BOOKS BY KATE HALEY

Welcome to the Inbetween

The Light After Earth

Like the Heroes of Old

Shilling & Florin Mysteries

1. The Jack of Hearts Murders

2. The Thief & the Marquis

3. A Dalliance with Grief

4. The Case of Silver & Sovereign

5. A Cold & Bitter Revenge

6. The Pen & the Blade

7. Blood & Bells

8. Tarnished Silver

The War of the North Saga

Footsteps into the Unfamiliar (short story collection)

1. Steel & Stone

2. Magic in the Marshes

3. Forest of Ghosts

4. Women of the Woods

5. Spirit & Sand

6. The Prince and the Witch

7. Gods & Dragons

The Vincent Temple Trilogy (+ Prequel)

Path of Dreaming Souls (Prequel)

1. Gateway to Dark Stars

2. Tomb of Endless Night

3. Fortress of the Shadow Reich

ABOUT THE AUTHOR

Kate Haley is a speculative fiction author who works predominantly in fantasy and horror.

While currently content to fill their days with writing and table-top RPGs, their grander plans involve world domination. Something akin to the tyranny of the greatest city atop the Disc would be an acceptable standard. They believe a super-villainous overlord would be an upgrade, given that our current villains lack style and imagination.

After all, super-villainy requires Presentation.

If you like their references, consider visiting their website www.katehaleyauthor.com for short fictions and merchandise, and join the mailing list for early access and exclusive cool stuff.

You can also get in touch through the website regarding their work, your position in future slave armies, or a general interest in all things nerdy and wonderful.

www.ingramcontent.com/pod-product-compliance
Lightning Source LLC
Chambersburg PA
CBHW061244310726
48971CB00007B/2213